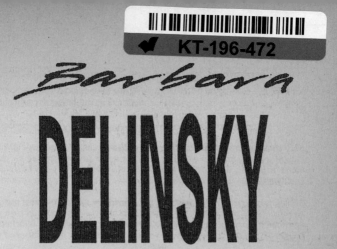

Barbara

DELINSKY

SECRET OF
THE STONE

MIRA BOOKS

*First published in Great Britain 1986
Reprinted in Great Britain 1995
by Mira Books*

© Barbara Delinsky 1985

ISBN 1 55166 113 6

58-9505

*Printed in Great Britain by
BPC Paperbacks Ltd*

1

"WHAT DO YOU THINK, Jesse?"

"Not bad. Not bad at all."

"Kinda pale?"

"May just be the lights. They're geared for sculpture, not skin."

"She does look sculpted."

"Nicely."

"Reedy."

"Hmm, no. Slender, maybe. But there are curves."

"You're searching."

"Aren't you, Ben? Isn't that why the two of us are standing here gawking at her, rather than at her artwork?"

"I suppose. Want to know what Margie says?"

"What does Margie say?"

"Margie says she's a loner. Cool and unattached. Reputed to be untouchable, almost like her work."

"I don't know. Her work is sensual in its way."

"Sensual? Are you kidding? Cold rock?"

"Come on, Ben. Where's your appreciation of art? She's done amazing things with marble. It may have been cold, hard stone once, but she's wrung something very warm from it."

"Hmph. Maybe so. But I think Margie might be right. Look at her. It's like she's insulated somehow from all this."

"And to her credit. How would *you* like to have two hundred people milling around scrutinizing you?"

"They're scrutinizing her work, Jesse, not *her*."

"Wanna bet? The exhibit's going to be on for the next four weeks. This is the only night the sculptress will be here. Don't tell me these people always choose to dress up in monkey suits in ninety-degree weather to go to a crowded gallery. Hell, I wouldn't be here myself if you hadn't dragged me."

"It's good for you."

"It's good for *you*. You're the guy who has to go places on the chance that you might pick up a client or two. You just want me along to add class. Whew, it's warm in here."

"It's air-conditioned."

"Yeah. But it's crowded, and besides, we had to go outside to get here. So did everyone else. Which proves my point. They're here to see *her*. No other reason."

"Hell, Jesse. This is the cream of New York society. These people dress up all the time. Besides, it's not *too* rough moving from an air-conditioned penthouse to an air-conditioned limo to an air-conditioned gallery. They don't suffer."

"Come to think of it, there were an awful lot of limousines out there."

"It's a narrow street."

"Man, she looks cool as a cuke."

"That's what I said."

"No. Cool as in composed...in control...
polished."

"Just like that alabaster figurine over there."

"It looks alive."

"But it's stone. So's she."

"That's where you're wrong, Ben. There's feeling in
her work. It may have a hard, shiny finish, but there's
feeling in it. I'd guess there's plenty of feeling in *her*."

"You're nuts. She's hard. Look at her —like porcelain."

"Mmm. Fragile. Very lovely."

"But inert. Dead."

"Nope. I'd say deep down inside she's a passionate
woman."

"Passionate? That's funny. Even if Margie hadn't
tipped me off, I'd have judged her to be frigid."

"Frigidity is relative, my friend. To you or me, a raw
piece of marble is frigid. To *her*, it has feeling...which
she has the skill to bring out. If she is reputedly untouchable, it may be because a man has never come
along who's skillful enough to chip through the outer
shell to find the warmth beneath. Mmm, I'd say she's a
very passionate woman."

"Is that smugness I hear? Come on, Jesse. You may
be the master of seduction, but she's not your type."

"No?"

"No. You like fast women. Glossy, sexy women."

"Umm. And after the act they leave me cold as ice."

"I'm telling you. That one'd be cold before, during
and after the act."

"Wanna bet?"

"Yeah, I'll bet. I'll bet you can't get to first base with her."

"He-ey, you underestimate the master."

"What'll you bet?"

"Hmm. Nice arms. Graceful. Too bad her legs are covered by that damned gown—they're probably the same."

"She may have sausage thighs."

"I doubt it. Look at her breasts—just suggestive enough beneath that silk . . ."

"Tickets to the play-offs?"

"Hmm?"

"I'll bet you a pair of tickets to the play-offs."

"The play-offs? Look who's talking speculation. You don't even know if the Knicks'll make it to the finals."

"They'll make it. I doubt you will."

"You're very sure of yourself."

"And you're not? Well, is it a bet?"

"I don't know, Ben. Good Knicks tickets are hard enough to get during the season."

"What's the matter, Jesse? Getting cold feet? Is the master having second thoughts?"

"Not on your life. She's penetrable. It just may take time. That kind of woman needs to be wooed."

"*Wooed*? Geez, you're going soft. Since when have you had to *woo* a woman?"

"This one's different. If I'm gonna do it, I'll have to do it right."

"You're chicken."

"No way."

"Two tickets to the play-offs?"

"The play-offs—*if* the Knicks are in them—will be only a week from now."

"A week is a long time . . . unless you're losing your touch."

"Not on your life."

"Two tickets?"

"Come to think of it, I would like to see the Knicks whip L.A. Wonder if the sculptress likes basketball."

"I'll be the one to win the tickets, pal."

"You won't win."

"Wanna bet?"

"You're on."

PAIGE MATTHESON stood serenely amid a cluster of admirers. She smiled and nodded, speaking softly when questioned about one piece or another that was on display. When the group shifted and several new faces approached, she began the ritual again. Franco Roget, the gallery owner, stayed close by her elbow and introduced her to everyone.

Her composure was exquisite. No one meeting her had the slightest inkling that she'd rather be elsewhere. No one meeting her would have imagined the convincing it had taken to get her here. She seemed perfectly at ease, if the slightest bit shy. But the shyness was appealing, adding to the alabaster beauty that was so much in keeping with her art.

"So you work exclusively in stone?" one patron asked.

"No. I also enjoy working with wood."

"I don't see any of those pieces here tonight," a second guest remarked.

"They're on display at other galleries around the city. We decided to limit this exhibit."

"Wood, stone—they're not the usual for a contemporary artist, are they?"

She smiled. "Many sculptors today work with newer media—metals, plastics, synthetics. But I think there's a slow but growing movement back to more traditional materials. The challenge is in taking the traditional and sculpting it into something thoroughly modern."

"You've done it well." This from a man who'd been introduced to her as Christopher Wright III. Though slightly shorter than she was—perhaps the same height had she been barefoot—he was reasonably good-looking." Are you as modern as your work?"

"I'm as traditional." It was her stock line for men who were fishing, and Christopher Wright III was fishing. If the heavy scent of his cologne hadn't warned her, his proprietorial stance by her side would have.

"How about a traditional dinner?" he murmured, leaning closer. "I understand you're going to be in the city for several days."

Her poise didn't waver. "Just one more, and it's booked up from start to finish. If all goes well, I'll be on my way home the day after tomorrow. I'm afraid I just won't have time, Mr. Wright—"

"Christopher. Do you get to New York often?" he asked.

She shook her head, then turned as another of the group asked where she lived. "I'm from New England. Not far away, but far enough. I don't think I'd ever get any work done if I lived in a city like this. The pace is mind-boggling." If she sounded like a small-town girl, it was by design. The fact was, she'd cut her teeth on Manhattan. From the time she'd been old enough to walk more than a block without complaining, her parents had taken her and her brothers on visits to the city. She'd always been glad to go home again.

As new people joined the group, others drifted away. In her quiet, understated way, Paige made impressions on each just as she was expected to do. She graciously handled small talk and discussed her work, deftly parried personal questions by smoothly shifting the conversation back to the moment.

At all times she appeared to give her full attention to the person to whom she was speaking, yet she was attuned to bits and snatches of conversations around her. Her work was being well received, and she was pleased. She also knew that, though her shyness was sometimes taken as aloofness, the group of patrons present had seemed to warm to her. As for the occasional derogatory comment, breathed behind her back by the Christopher Wright IIIs of the crowd after they'd made their play and failed, she shunted the hurt aside. Oh, yes, she knew what they thought. "Ice maiden" was a term she'd heard more than once. She didn't know if the label was true, only knew that she hadn't yet laid eyes on the man with whom she cared to put it to a test.

IT WAS LATE THAT NIGHT when the crowd finally dispersed. Soon after, Paige found herself in a small restaurant with her agent Marjory Goodwin, and Marjory's assistant, Carolyn Pook.

Marjory twirled her wineglass, sat back in her seat with an exaggerated sigh and grinned broadly. "We did it, ladies. That was quite a success. Of course, a third of the pieces on display are on loan from private collections, but if the queries pan out, we may have sold fully half of the rest."

"You're kidding," Paige said. Surprise and pleasure were quick antidotes for her fatigue. "That many?"

"Yup. That many... *if* the queries pan out."

"They should," Carolyn interjected. "At least, if the enthusiasm of the people I spoke with is any indication. They loved your stuff, Paige. Congratulations."

Paige smiled warmly. "Thanks. I hope they did. I don't think I can manage these trips often."

"You look bushed," Marjory observed.

"I couldn't sleep last night. The city keys me up."

"The town house is comfortable, isn't it? Sylvia said to make yourself at home."

"Oh, it's lovely. And it was kind of your friend to offer it. But making oneself at home is one thing. Being at home is another. I miss the ocean."

"You've only been gone a day."

"I know. But it's soothing there. The endless roll of the surf is very different from the eternal ruckus here. You've been to my house, Margie. You know how peaceful it is."

"Hmph. I'm a city girl. The ocean is a nice place to visit, but to live there? The peace would drive me mad."

"Don't you get lonesome?" Carolyn asked. "You live there all alone."

"It's the only way I can work. And I like living alone. Besides, there's always the surf. When I wake up in the middle of the night I go out on the deck. I can't imagine a sedative more effective than that soothing rhythm."

"I can," Marjory drawled, arching her brows suggestively. "Another rhythm. One as timeless."

Carolyn laughed. "Marjory Goodwin, you have a one-track mind."

"It's a wild track, isn't it? Let me tell you, there were some good-looking men there tonight. If I hadn't been so busy trying to sell your work, Paige, I might have been tempted to make use of Franco's private room at the back of the gallery."

"It was in use," Carolyn informed her blithely. "I saw Craig Hutchinson go in there with his date. Craig must wield some clout with Franco."

"I thought they wielded it together," Marjory remarked dryly. "Unless Craig's suddenly gone straight. In which case Franco should have been distraught."

"Franco was as preoccupied as you were," Paige pointed out. "He was really wonderful, staying so close beside me all night."

Carolyn laughed. "Maybe he was trying to make Craig jealous. But again that doesn't fit. By rights, if he wanted to make Craig jealous, he should have hung on the arm of some gorgeous guy." She frowned. "Unless we've really screwed up this analysis."

Paige sipped her wine, then set it down as her companions continued to discuss the relationship between Franco and Craig. "Poor Franco. How does he ever put up with you two?"

"He loves us," Marjory answered. "That's one of the things that's so great about him. He's not threatened by women as many men are." She lowered her voice. "Did you get a chance to meet Tom Chester? Big guy, but all muscle, no fat?"

"How would you know it's muscle?" Carolyn teased.

Marjory grinned. "I managed to put my arm around his waist. You know how agents can be when they're trying to sell something. And that waist was lean." Again she lowered her voice. "I gave him my card. Just in case he wants . . . anything."

Paige laughed aloud. If she didn't know Marjory Goodwin as well as she did, she'd have been offended by the definitely unprofessional turn of the conversation. But she did know her. Marjory happened to be wonderfully kind and solicitous to her. Marjory happened to be utterly effective, a whiz at selling her work. Marjory also happened, at the age of forty, to be man hungry. "You're incorrigible, Margie. What happened to David?"

"David? Oh, David's fine. He said to send his regrets. He had a business meeting tonight or he would have been at the gallery."

"Wouldn't he mind if you just picked up and had an affair with another man?"

"Sure he would."

"Then . . . why all this talk?"

Leaning forward, Marjory patted Paige's hand. "Because it's talk. And it's fun. And David, for all those boring business meetings of his, still happens to be a fantastic lover. I'm telling you, Paige, you really should get yourself a man. It'd open all kinds of new horizons."

Paige sat back and gave her friend a self-confident smile. "My horizons are plenty wide, thank you. I like my life just the way it is."

It was Carolyn's turn to lean forward. "But think of how much more exciting it could be." her eyes widened. "You could fly off for the weekend every now and again with some handsome prince. There were several there tonight."

"Princes?" Paige laughed. "Carolyn, Carolyn, I think you've spent too much time with Margie. Either that or you're still hung up on fairy tales, which, since you're nearly my age, I doubt. Margie, what are you doing to this poor girl?"

"This poor girl," Marjory scoffed, "has had the time of her life these past few months escorting some of our most attractive clients around town. She's got Walter Emerson calling her twice a week."

"The cartoonist? But I thought he was in his fifties!"

"Careful, dear," Marjory said. "To some of us, fifty doesn't sound that old."

"You're off by a decade, anyway," Carolyn corrected Paige. "People make the mistake all the time. It's because of his name—"

"And that gray hair—"

"Prematurely gray. More like thick, gleaming silver." Carolyn's grin told far more than her words. "He's a nice guy."

"And has he whisked you away to— Doesn't he live in some huge plantation house in South Carolina?"

"Georgia. And it's beautiful. But we're getting off the subject."

"Which is?"

"Finding you a man."

Paige turned from Carolyn to Marjory. "Tell her, Margie."

"Tell her what?" Marjory countered innocently.

"That I'm not interested."

Eyeing Paige's placid smile, Marjory scowled. "Well, you should be. You're twenty-nine years old and it's about time you *experienced* life."

"I've experienced plenty."

Her protest was ignored. Marjory narrowed her gaze on Carolyn. "How about Jon Whitley? He's a runner. He's in great shape."

Carolyn tipped her head, thoughtfully looking at Paige. "Hmm. Maybe. But I dunno—his hair's just her color. I think we need some contrast here."

"I'm not interested," Paige stated.

"Bill Shaeffer," Carolyn counteroffered. "The coloring's right, and the guy's newly divorced—"

"For the third time. Chalk him."

"I'm not interested," Paige repeated, though for all the good it did she might have been the only one to hear the three small words.

Just then Marjory's eyes lit up. "I know. Donovan Greene!"

Paige sent a gaze heavenward. "Spare me, Lord. I've done no wrong—"

"That's just the point, Paige," Marjory stated. "You're *too* good. It's about time you break out and do something—" she struggled for the words "—something daring." She gave a vicarious shiver of delight. "What you need is to find a terrific-looking guy and have a hot, bone-melting, blood-pumping affair. It's good for the soul, Paige. Good for the soul."

Paige sincerely doubted it. Her indulgent smile said as eloquently as anything could that she didn't for a minute take Marjory seriously. And by the time the chauffeured limousine finally dropped her back at the borrowed town house and she was alone at last, she was too tired to give much thought to anything but showering and falling into bed.

AWAKENING RELUCTANTLY to the sound of her alarm, Paige struggled to roll out of bed the next morning. Exhaustion had overcome urban insomnia; she'd been dead to the world for hours. Though usually a morning person, she felt less than chipper. She was not looking forward to the day, one in which she would be hopping from one gallery to another, visiting the dealers who sold her work.

She showered again, more to shake the morning muzzies and relax herself than to clean the body that had been thoroughly cleaned the night before. Wearing a soft silk teddy, she sat at the dressing table and brushed her thick, dark hair before gathering and pinning it into a shiny knot at her nape. This, too, was a reluctant move. At home she let her hair fall loose, enjoying the sensual feel of the gentle waves at her shoulders. Here in New York, though, her hairstyle reflected her city image—sleek, controlled, elegantly poised. She needed to look older, sophisticated. She knew that of the people she'd be seeing today there would be those who might resent the fact that she'd found success at the tender age of twenty-nine.

In keeping with this purpose, she carefully applied makeup to cover the faint sprinkling of freckles across the bridge of her nose. The sun had brought them out in early spring, and had later deepened them. Given her habit of taking daily walks on the beach, freckles had been unavoidable. Not that she normally minded them; she felt they added spice to her face, giving her a natural, healthy look. Unfortunately, it wasn't the look she wanted today.

Finishing off her makeup with graded shades of lavender eye shadow, then dark liner and mascara, she feathered a shadow of blusher on her cheeks, then stood. Staring at herself in the mirror, she had to admit her success. She did look mature, quite sophisticated. Her preference for no makeup could wait. One more day, that was all. One more day.

Wearing a summer suit of white linen with a black silk blouse beneath, she made a final analysis of her appearance in the bedroom's full-length mirror. *Not bad, Paige,* she thought. *Mother would be pleased.* Not only had she attained the overall effect she'd wanted, but she did feel properly dressed for the city. It was something that had been ingrained in her from the earliest age. She remembered the discussions vividly.

"No, Paige, you may *not* wear jeans."

"But the boys are wearing them."

"The boys are different. And they'll be wearing blazers, which will dress them up. A young lady does not wear dungarees in Manhattan. That's all there is to it."

So it had been decreed; so it was. Paige smiled fondly at the thought of her very elegant, very proper mother. They'd always gotten along well, partly because, for all her elegance, her mother loved her dearly. That fact had never been disguised. And Paige had quickly learned to compromise. Indeed, she probably wouldn't feel comfortable wearing slacks in the city now, though so many women did. Dressing up was something of a novelty for her, anyway, since at home she wore what she wanted when she wanted. And by the following evening she'd be free....

If only there weren't this odious business of forcing smiles for ofttimes boring gallery owners!

Glancing at the slim gold watch on her wrist, she saw that her driver was due in twenty minutes. She headed downstairs to the kitchen, then brewed herself a cup of coffee, perching on a high stool at the counter to drink it. If she were at home, she mused, she'd have coffee on the deck, then disappear into her studio for several hours' work before emerging for breakfast. Today there wouldn't be such a lovely midmorning break, and it occurred to her that she ought to scramble an egg. But her stomach rebelled. She simply could not eat at eight forty-five in the morning. She'd have to wait for lunch—wherever and whenever that would be.

Returning to the upstairs bedroom with coffee cup in hand, she sprayed cologne on her neck, her wrists, then into the air, promptly walking through the fragrant cloud. Carrying both her purse and the coffee, she descended the two flights to the living room to await the limousine.

She still had five minutes to spare. As always, she was early. With the painfully slow passing of seconds, she began to curse the habit. Idleness bred contemplation, and contemplation this day centered on the meetings ahead.

"Margie, you know how I hate those things," she'd protested over the phone the week before.

"I know, which is why I haven't told you about them until now. The less time you have to brood, the better off you'll be. But Paige, they want to see you, especially the gallery owners who are handling your work for the first time."

"Why can't they just come to the opening?"

"They can, and many of them will be there. But the opening is mostly for patrons and those dealers who can make it in from out of town. The local dealers take pride in their own galleries, and you really can't blame them. It'll be a feather in their caps to have you there, even for an hour. And you make such a good impression."

"At great cost. By the end of the day, my mouth will be stiff from smiling and my legs will ache from all that standing."

"So ask them for a chair."

"Won't you be with me?"

"No. Not that day. The limousine will pick you up. The driver will have your schedule. At the end of the day he'll sweep by to collect me and we'll have dinner together. You'll be able to tell me how everything went."

"Coward."

"Now, now, none of that. You'll do better on your own, Paige. The owners will be very proprietorial."

"That's what I'm afraid of. Really, Margie, I wish you hadn't planned a full day."

"Once a year...is that too much to ask? It's for a good cause, Paige. Your career's flourishing. This will give it an added boost."

"I'd rather let my work stand on its own."

"I know you would, and it does. But a little back-scratching now and again doesn't hurt."

A little back-scratching. Just what Paige hated. There was a phoniness about it that rankled her. If she had to stay in New York another day, she'd much rather have spent it going to museums or even shopping. Of course, her preference would have been to drive home that very morning.

Feeling uncharacteristically testy, and resenting the cause of her mood, she downed the last of her coffee just as the front doorbell rang. Nine o'clock. Felix was always on time . . . damn him.

Snatching her purse from the cushion beside her, she pushed herself up, telling herself that she shouldn't take her sour mood out on the poor man whose job was to shuttle her from gallery to gallery for the next ten hours. A quick glance out the window revealed the familiar lines of the long, black limousine. Assured that the bell indeed announced her driver, she opened the door with a flourish, only to catch her breath when she saw that the man awaiting her was most definitely not Felix. Felix was a small man with sparse gray hair. The man before her, though he wore a similar dark suit, white shirt and tie, was tall, broad-shouldered and lean. His skin was faintly tanned, his sandy hair obviously full beneath his very proper chauffeur's cap. But it was his eyes that drew and held Paige's gaze. They were blue, crystal-clear and strangely refreshing.

"Ms. Mattheson?" he asked in a deep voice that was a bit gravelly.

"Yes?" She was aware of a rush of warmth and wondered if it was going to be another scorching day.

"My name is Dallas. I'll be your driver for the day."

His eyes danced; she couldn't look away. With great effort she controlled a sudden breathlessness. "I . . . is Felix ill?"

"The agency needed him for something else today. I have a complete list of your stops." He glanced past her toward the living room, freeing Paige's eyes from his own compelling ones. "Is there anything you need to bring with you?"

"Just my purse." Unnecessarily, she held it up. "I'm all set."

"Then I'd suggest we start out. The traffic's pretty heavy." He reached to close the door behind her as she passed him.

At the close contact, Paige realized just how large he was. At five foot five—more, given her heels—she'd never thought of herself as being short. This man, she decided, was six-two at least. Six-two, and built. *So there, Marjory Goodwin, I did notice!*

"It's going to be pretty hot again," came the voice by her side. "Unusual for the first of June."

"It is," she said softly as she climbed the few stairs that led up to the street. Dallas was instantly before her, opening the rear door of the limousine. She thanked him and settled herself into the seat while he slid behind the wheel. He checked what had to be her schedule on the seat beside him, then started the car.

"You've got a busy day," he commented, sparing her a glance in his rearview mirror moments before he pulled away from the curb.

"Mmm. I'll say." But her voice held little of the annoyance she'd felt moments before. The appearance of this man had broken the momentum of her ill mood; she felt decidedly better than she had before he'd come.

They drove in silence. Paige removed her own copy of her schedule from her purse and studied it in preparation for her first stop. When they arrived at the small East Side gallery, Dallas pulled over to the curb, hopped out and opened the door for her.

"I'll be right here waiting for you," he said as he accompanied her to the gallery door and held it open.

She tipped up her head and smiled. Moments later she was being effusively greeted by the first of those whose backs she'd come to scratch.

When she emerged from the gallery an hour later, Dallas was lounging against the side of the limousine. At the sight of her, he immediately straightened and jumped to open the door.

"How did it go?" he asked, his rough voice soothing. Again Paige had the sensation of a breath of fresh air.

She rolled her eyes and said nothing, but the corners of her lips twitched as she slid into the back of the car.

"Sorry about the heat," he said. "I started the car to cool it off every so often, but it's a losing battle on a day like this." He switched the air conditioner to high.

"This is fine." Paige felt simple relief at being away from the cloying atmosphere of the gallery. As the car headed off, she studied her driver. His hair was neatly trimmed at his neck, shorter at the sideburns as was the style. She couldn't help wondering if he wouldn't be cooler without the hat; it seemed a shame to imprison such thick hair in any way.

Redirecting her wayward thoughts, she reviewed the past hour. It hadn't been all that bad. Henry Thistle had enthusiastically shown her how her pieces had been set out for display. He had gone into detailed discourse on the sales he'd made in the past few months and the homes he'd found for her work. In turn, she had exhibited due appreciation and gratitude, stroking the man with gentle praise, admiring the works of other artists in his shop. No, it hadn't been all that bad, but eight more such stops before the day was done?

"Here we go." Dallas tossed his head toward the gallery they approached.

"Already?" She was cool and comfortable and would have preferred to drive around for a while.

"'Fraid so," he returned. There was something mischievous in the gaze he sent back to her, something that underscored his insightfulness. She had little time to ponder it, though, for he had parked and was helping her out, again assuring her that he'd be waiting.

He was. This time she simply nodded and sank into the back seat to recover from her second appointment. This one had been downright boring. The gallery owner had been a quiet, dignified man who had handled only two of her pieces. After fifteen minutes she hadn't known quite what to say to him. It had been a relief that Marjory, wisely, had only allotted him forty-five minutes. As it was, she'd made her escape after forty.

"Are you okay?"

She looked up to find that, rather than shutting her door, Dallas was leaning in, his blue eyes strangely clouded. "I'm okay," she said quietly, then took a deep breath and steeled herself. "I'm okay."

Though he looked doubtful, he returned to his place behind the wheel and started off again. "Are you sure you'll make it through seven more stops?" he called gently over his shoulder when they had stopped at a light.

"I'd better or Margie will have my head."

"Margie?"

"My agent. She's the one who set up these meetings for me."

The light turned green and the limousine moved forward. "Do you have work in all of these galleries?"

She chuckled. "I'm not *that* prolific. I've got things in five of the nine. The other four are future possibilities."

Nodding, Dallas gave full attention to guiding the car smoothly through the crowded streets. Paige had the sudden impulse to ask him about himself, but she curbed it, knowing that a certain distance was traditionally kept between driver and passenger in limousines of this length. Besides, it was enough that she felt his touch each time he glanced in the rearview mirror, that her hand tingled each time he helped her out of the car, that the sight of him when she emerged from an appointment was instant resuscitation. She didn't need to breach *too* many boundaries.

After the third gallery had been visited, Paige sagged back against the seat. The owner she'd spoken with had been a woman, polite enough but with an aggressiveness that made Paige uncomfortable. Her own manner was so much more easygoing, yet she'd left that gallery feeling that she had to rush home to work round the clock for the next few months to provide the pieces that the woman insisted she already had buyers for. Such confidence should have been encouraging, but it served only to make Paige tense. Once again she realized that she could never, never live in the city.

"How about a cold drink?" Dallas offered. "The next stop is nearby. We've got a few minutes to spare."

Lifting her head from where it lolled against the seat, Paige brightened. "That's the best offer I've had all morning." She saw the bunching of Dallas's cheek and knew he was smiling.

"Done."

Within minutes he'd pulled up at an umbrella-shaded stand at the corner. Leaning across his seat, he studied the billboard.

"Looks like it's all in cans. What'll it be—Coke, 7 UP, orange soda?"

"Coke will be fine." *Anything* to soothe her dry throat and give her a bit of energy. She reached to take money from her purse, but Dallas was out of the car before she could press the bills in his hand. Through the dark glass of the limousine windows, she watched him speak to the vendor, then dig into his pocket. The movement brushed his jacket aside and pulled the fabric of his slacks smoothly across a thigh that was firm and well formed.

Paige blushed, unable to fathom where her sudden interest in the male physique had come from. Dallas was her driver, for heaven's sake! Her *chauffeur*!

By the time he returned, she'd recomposed herself. He slid into the driver's seat and twisted to hand her the drink. She noted that he'd bought one for himself and felt a twinge of guilt that he had to wait out in the heat while she went from one air-conditioned gallery to another. He looked cool enough, however, with only a faint sheen of dampness on his neck to suggest that he might be warm.

She thrust the money forward. "Here." At his blank look, she explained. "For the drinks. Both of them."

For a split second he seemed almost angry. His brows lowered, his mouth settled into a firm line. Then he relaxed his features. "Thank you, but it'll be taken care of by the agency." His eyes met hers with that same devastating lure that could capture her, sweep her up and set her on a brighter plane.

She forced herself to nod and lowered her head to return the money to her purse, then accepted the cold drink and settled back in her seat. Dallas pulled around one corner, then another until he found a shady spot to stop the car. Only then did he snap open the tab of his Coke. Lifting the can to his mouth, he tipped his head back and took a long swallow. From her perch behind him, slightly to his right, Paige followed the path of the liquid, watching the muscles of his throat constrict to carry it down. His sudden "Oh!" snapped her to attention. Reaching into the pocket of his jacket, he pulled out a straw and passed it to her.

His sheepish expression was thoroughly endearing, making her smile. "Thanks. I think you had the right idea the first time."

But she accepted the straw. If she were at home, she would never have bothered with it. Unfortunately, she wasn't at home. She was in the middle of Manhattan, ensconced in the roomy hollow of a sleek limousine. So instead she carefully peeled off the wrapper and inserted the straw into the flip-top opening of the can. When she looked up she saw Dallas studying her, faint amusement in his eyes. With a shrug, she began to sip her drink.

Moments later she sighed. "Ahhhh, that's better."

"Don't they offer refreshments at your meetings?"

"Hot coffee. Or tea, equally hot. Not terribly creative, or welcome on a day like this. I think there must be something etched in the gallery owner's manual to the extent that boiling water is a must. It doesn't impress *me* terribly much, but then . . ." She let her voice trail off, realizing that Dallas might think her less sophisticated than her image.

But he smiled and turned to the front, saying nothing at all to reveal his opinion of her. As she thought about it, she was surprised—though pleased—that he'd gotten himself a drink. Somehow chauffeurs always seemed immune to the needs of mortals. She was relieved that Dallas was not.

All too soon they'd finished their drinks and she was headed for her fourth appointment. It and the fifth were a repeat of the earlier ones, with the exception of several collectors of her work being present at each. Paige wore her most composed expression, conversed as smoothly as she had the night before and was drained once again when she finally relaxed in the limousine. It was nearly two o'clock.

"You look tired," Dallas remarked, turning in his seat to study her pale features before starting the car. "I hope they fed you."

She shook her head, then wearily laid the back of her hand against her warm brow. "Each assumed I'd been fed elsewhere. Evidently gallery owners' manuals don't go into ensuring an artist's survival."

Instead of smiling at her humor, Dallas continued to examine her closely. There was a grim set to his lips, not unlike earlier, when she'd offered to pay for their drinks. Then he turned and started the car. "We'll have to remedy that." Maneuvering the long limousine out into the traffic, he followed the flow, making one deft turn then another before finally pulling up before a small restaurant. "I'll be right back," he said abruptly. Warm as it was with the car turned off, Paige was grateful to simply sit and rest.

When he returned, he carried a large brown bag. Bidden by hunger and an enthusiasm sparked by promise of its assuagement, she flipped down one of the folding chairs and slid forward onto it. "What have you got?"

He headed out into the traffic again. "This 'n' that. Any objection to the park? If there's any breeze it'll be there, and we can at least get some shade and a little quiet for you."

Touched by his concern, she smiled. "The park sounds wonderful. But I didn't think there were places to stop."

"Not to the uninitiated, perhaps," he drawled in such exaggerated fashion that she had to laugh. A far cry from the eminently controlled Felix. She was glad Dallas was with her today. Propping a forearm against the back of the front seat, she watched him drive. It didn't occur to her to return to her own place.

"You're a native New Yorker?" she asked.

"No. But I've been here long enough to find little ins and outs that many people miss."

"Of course. Your job. You must know these streets like the back of your hand."

He didn't answer for a minute. Then he spoke in a pensive tone. "Perhaps it's in spite of my job. There are times when I feel I'm stuck here and I need a reminder that there are, in fact, open spaces in the world. Central Park is far from what I crave, but when one is desperate and without recourse, second best will do."

There was such sincerity in his voice that Paige knew he was speaking person-to-person rather than chauffeur-to-passenger. He spoke well. She wondered where he'd come from, what he'd done in life, why he'd chosen to become a chauffeur. He looked to be in his late thirties. There were tiny lines around his eyes—whether from laughing or squinting, she didn't know—and the ghost of creases by the corners of his mouth. She remembered how he'd frowned when he'd been studying her earlier, and realized that those creases had perfectly fit the frown. He was a man who had many a sober moment, she sensed, and she continued to wonder about him as they approached the park. To her amazement, he found a small turnoff from one of the park roads and crept along it for just a minute before pulling to a halt beneath a stand of trees.

"This is terrific," she exclaimed as he helped her from the back. He held her hand firmly in his as he too surveyed the bit of peace they'd found, then slowly released it.

"Let me get the things." Ducking into the car, he picked up the bag, tossing his hat onto the seat in exchange. He had only half straightened when he cast a hesitant look her way. "You don't mind, do you?"

"Of course not. I was wondering if you were hot wearing it."

Tucking the bag under his arm, he raked his hair from his forehead with his free hand. Paige could see that it was damp, also that it had been shaped by a fine barber. It fell promptly into place, full and vibrant.

Realizing she was staring, she averted her gaze under the pretense of finding a place to sit. Dallas appeared to be doing the same, for moments later he gestured to a spot where the grass was thick and soft.

"There. That should do just fine." He glanced back at Paige, dropping his gaze to her white skirt. "Uh, on second thought, we may have a problem here. You look so pretty and neat. Grass stains would never do." Then he gave her a slow, lazy grin. Before she could begin to imagine what solution he had in mind, he'd thrust the bag containing their lunch at her and had shrugged out of his jacket. Covering the distance to the chosen spot with three long strides, he spread the jacket on the ground with a gallant flourish. His smile was broad when he straightened and extended his hand.

Paige felt strangely reckless, as though she was breaking a rule being here with her chauffeur this way. But Dallas was more relaxing than anyone she'd been with in the past two days. And although an air-conditioned restaurant might certainly have been cooler, this spot promised to be more quiet. Besides, if she went to a restaurant, Dallas would wait in the car. It struck her that for the first time in recent memory she wanted the company.

2

SEATED COMFORTABLY on Dallas's jacket, Paige watched him unpack their lunch.

"Crabmeat. Chilled shrimp. Fresh fruit salad. Pita bread." He identified the contents of each container as he set it on the grass. "And lemonade with extra ice." He drew paper plates, plastic forks and a wad of napkins from the bag and was about to uncover the first container when he paused. "Tell me you're allergic to fish."

She laughed, feeling oddly lighthearted. "Living on the water the way I do? I play games with myself. If I accomplish what I want on a particular day, the reward is a quick ride into town to pick up fresh fish from the dock. Lobster, shrimp, cod—whatever they've got, I eat."

Prying the lid off the crabmeat salad, he scooped healthy dollops onto each plate. "You live on the water?"

"Uh-huh. Marblehead Neck. It's on the north shore of Massachusetts."

"Near Gloucester."

Her eyes brightened. "You're familiar with the area?"

"I have friends there." He divided the shrimp evenly between them. "I try to get up whenever I can. It's a beautiful area."

"I know. I love it."

"Have you always lived there?"

"No. My family's from Connecticut. But I'd visited Marblehead as a child and when it came to finding a place of my own I knew just where I wanted to go."

He sat back to study her for a minute, then reached for the fresh fruit and doled it out. "It's an inspiring area. Must be conducive to working, if the number of artists there is any indication."

"It's perfect. The Sausalito of the East Coast." For the first time she glanced down at her plate. "Hey, that's enough. I'm not sure I can eat all you've given me."

His gaze was knowing. "When was the last time you ate?"

"Last night."

"Then you'll eat it all." His lips twitched. "And anything you can't, I'll help you with. I have a passion for shrimp. In fact, you'd better start. I've been known to snitch from other people's plates even *before* they've had their fill."

She glanced at her watch, then, her expression sobering, reached for her plate. "Hmm. We haven't got all that much time anyway." Within seconds a twinkle returned to her eye. "I think I'll start on the shrimp." Picking one up, she dipped it into the sauce Dallas presented. "Mmmmmm. Not bad . . . for New York."

"I'll have you know we get the best of fresh fish here."

"Not as fresh as my dock."

He dipped into the cocktail sauce himself. "You're prejudiced. If you were to close your eyes right now and picture yourself on that dock surrounded by the salty

air and the sounds of fishermen unloading their catch,
I doubt you'd taste a difference in the shrimp."

She knew he was right. Even without closing her eyes
and transporting herself to the seaside, she found the
shrimp to be delicious. It had to be the atmosphere here,
she decided, tipping her head back to scan the green-
ery overhead.

"There is a little breeze. I didn't think there was any."
Realizing that she still wore her linen jacket, she wiped
her fingers on a napkin, slipped out of the jacket and
laid it neatly on the grass beside her before reaching for
her lemonade. "This is nice. I didn't expect to have any
break at all." Her eyes sought his. "Thank you."

But his eyes weren't on hers. They were focused on
the strand of pearls that burrowed against the folds of
her black silk blouse. "Those are beautiful," he said
softly.

Self-conscious, she peered down at the pearls. "My
city beads. I never wear them at home."

"You don't dress up there?"

"Oh, occasionally, I suppose. To go into Boston from
time to time. But I much prefer to live casually."

"And you weren't thrilled about making this trip into
the city." He'd obviously put two and two together.

"No." Her voice was soft, almost apologetic.

"I'd think it would be exciting for you. I...understand
you're a very successful sculptress."

"My works are selling, yes. But the business side of
it all doesn't thrill me. These trips are tedious." She
watched him take a forkful of crabmeat. His hands were
strong, fingers well formed, slightly tanned, thoroughly masculine. She reached for another shrimp. "If

I had my way, I'd simply stay at home and let Margie do that selling on her own. For that matter," she thought aloud, "I wouldn't care if my pieces *ever* sold. It's the work itself that I love."

"But if you didn't sell, you wouldn't be able to support yourself. Uh, unless there's a man in the picture...."

"No man. And my needs aren't great." It was the truth, though not fully revealing. The fact was that she had a handsome inheritance from her parents, which would easily support her whether she sold her work or not. She knew how fortunate she was. It had occurred to her more than once, as her career had taken off, that the freedom she felt toward her work, the lack of monetary worry, might be in itself responsible for her artistic blossoming. Her life was tension free, so her work flowed.

"Don't you get lonesome up there all by yourself?" Dallas asked, repeating Carolyn's question of the night before almost verbatim. All too well, Paige recalled the aspects of that conversation dealing with men and sex. Looking at her chauffeur, so very handsome here beneath the oaks of Central Park, she felt a renewed twinge of the sensual awareness that had hit her from time to time since she'd opened her door that morning to gaze into the bluest of blue eyes. Stunned, she returned her attention to her lunch and gave Dallas the same answer she'd given Carolyn.

"I like being alone. It's the best way to work."

"But to play? What do you do for fun?"

She speared a cantaloupe cube. "My work is fun. And I have friends. There are parties sometimes. Small get-togethers." She raised her eyes to deny the defensiveness she'd heard in her own voice. "I walk the beach a lot. That's play. It's fun and relaxing. I read. I window-shop in town. I take long drives along the coast. I may be alone, but I'm not lonely."

For a split second Paige caught the glint of skepticism in his gaze and thought he would argue. Seeming to curb the impulse, though, he took a bite of pita bread and lounged back on his elbows, crossing his long legs before him.

"This is nice," he mused, closing his eyes and breathing deeply.

Looking at him was so pleasant that she felt light-headed once more. "Mmm," she teased. "You do know the right spots, though I can't imagine that it'd be as charming at night."

His grin was crooked. He didn't open his eyes. "If you're suggesting that I bring my dates here to neck, you're wrong."

"I wouldn't suggest something like that," she drawled, knowing that was exactly what she'd done. "But now that you've mentioned it . . ."

"I come here myself. My dates prefer greater comfort."

"Then you're not married."

"No."

"Have you been driving long?"

"Since I was sixteen."

"I mean . . ." She gestured toward the limousine, slightly disconcerted that Dallas had stopped eating and was looking at her. She felt vulnerable to his gaze. Vulnerable . . . and almost as if she were being physically touched. Long, soothing fingers on her cheeks, her lips. A palm against the sensitive cord on the side of her neck.

"Oh, that," Dallas said. It took Paige a minute to recall that she'd asked him about his job. "No, not for very long. But it's proving to be an adventure. One way to meet interesting people."

"Tell me about them . . . the others you've driven around."

He sucked in a deep breath and sat up straight again. "I think we'd be better to concentrate on eating. You've got another appointment in twenty minutes."

At the reminder, she crinkled her nose. He seemed mesmerized by the gesture. "You've got freckles."

"Uh-oh. They were supposed to be covered up."

"Whatever for?"

"To make me look older."

"What are you, anyway?" His eyes were dancing again. "Thirty-three, thirty-four?"

A husky laugh rumbled from her throat. "I'm not sure whether to be thrilled or hurt. I'm twenty-nine."

"Imagine that," he said in mock wonder.

She shot him a quelling glance and stabbed a piece of honeydew with her fork. They ate in silence for a bit. Paige couldn't help but reflect on how comfortable she felt. There was something totally unhurried about Dallas, something about his relaxed manner that set her at ease. She knew full well that he was being paid for every minute of his time, but she didn't care. Even taken at face value, his solicitousness was good for her peace of mind.

As he'd predicted, she managed to do a respectable job on the food he'd dished out. It was with reluctance that she drained the last of her lemonade.

"I'm done, I guess." When she began to gather the plates together, the strong hand she'd admired moments before shot forward to rescue the lone shrimp that remained on her plate. As he dipped it in cocktail sauce and popped it into his mouth, he winked. Paige thought she'd melt. To control the sensation, she worked harder at cleaning up their impromptu picnic. But Dallas removed the plates from her hand, insisting on doing the dirty work himself while she stood, straightened her skirt and donned her jacket once more. That done, she picked up his jacket, shook it out, then draped it over her arm as she watched him walk to a rusty trash can and execute a graceful dropshot.

"Not bad," she teased. "Tell me you're an off-season basketball player."

"Off-season? But the season's not done."

"No?"

"No." He reached for the jacket she held out and shrugged into it. "The play-offs are still in progress. If I were a Knick, I'd be beating my tail up and down the court, praying for a chance to meet the Lakers in the finals." Placing a light hand at her waist, he guided her toward the car.

"Would you make it?" she asked in a breathy tone. Looking up, she caught his arched brows and a hint of amusement they gave his expression.

"I might. I just might at that."

THE NEXT FOUR HOURS, with one stop apiece, were even more exhausting for Paige than the earlier ones had been, for there was a strange restlessness in her that set patience at a premium. Overall she was pleased with the way she handled herself; she certainly had to be pleased with the reception she was given at each of the galleries she visited.

The brightest moments, though, came when she returned to the car. Dallas was her guardian angel, handing her in with care, making sure she was comfortable before he headed off. He was concerned by her fatigue and purposely took roundabout routes to prolong the drive from one stop to the next, sensing that she'd welcome the rest, which she did. She welcomed his frequent glances in the mirror, feeling strangely protected. She welcomed his intermittent discussion, which tapered off as soon as he sensed she needed a moment of quiet. She welcomed the ice-cream bar he thrust into her hand when she was almost wilting.

Increasingly, as the afternoon wore on, she found herself reacting to him. He had simply to approach her and she felt her insides tingle. And that was *before* he touched her arm or took her hand. Outside one of the galleries, her heel had caught in a sidewalk grate; he'd been there to catch her when she'd wobbled, and she'd clung to his strength for a long, precious moment.

He might have been her chauffeur, but he somehow seemed more like a friend. It was as though they shared an understanding of the day's ordeal, exchanging wry glances when a new gallery owner would greet her ebulliently. They might have been co-conspirators, stealing off to the park for lunch, clandestinely licking chocolate-covered ice-cream bars behind the shade of the limousine's dark glass.

Was she truly physically attracted to him? She tried to deny it, blaming the rush of warmth through her veins on the heat of the day. She tried to attribute her hormonal activity to the power of suggestion; having spent several hours the night before in the company of two such lecherous females as Marjory Goodwin and Carolyn Pook, it would be understandable if some of the hunger wore off.

Hunger? Paige Mattheson had never known sexual hunger before. She wasn't a virgin, though her one experience with a man, a fellow artist named Tyler Walsh, who'd been as young as she at the time, had ended with a total absence of satisfaction on her part. She'd never been inclined to try again. But then, she'd never, even that first time, felt the kind of inner excitement she felt now. It was as though hidden parts of her had suddenly come to life, as though the pulsing of her body demanded she recognize those heretofore ignored nooks and crannies.

Marjory's words came back to her and, for the first time, Paige wondered what it *would* be like to have a hot, bone-melting, blood-pumping affair. Would it be good for the soul? She wondered . . .

"Miss Goodwin said she'd be waiting at the door of her building at eight," Dallas announced as he turned onto Third Avenue, then cast a sharp glance in the mirror at Paige's face. "Are you sure you're up to this?"

"The worst is over," she answered quietly. "Margie will want a full rundown. I've got one more appointment tomorrow morning, then," she said, sighing, "I'll be on my way home."

"You're taking the shuttle to Boston?"

"No. I, uh, I have this thing about flying. It was one of the conditions I made when I agreed to come to the city. Felix drove me down the other day. I assume he'll be driving me back tomorrow."

Dallas said nothing as he pulled up at a modern structure fronted by smoky glass. Marjory breezed out almost simultaneously, jumping into the back seat with a sigh of relief.

"It is hot!" she exclaimed as she settled into the cool interior of the limousine. "I mean, it's not that everything isn't air-conditioned, but I've been running in and out all day and the constant switch is enervating." Rummaging in her voluminous bag, she extracted a tiny pillbox, tossed two aspirin into her mouth and swallowed.

Paige winced. "You can do that without water?"

"Since we have no water and I have a splitting headache, yes." She directed her voice toward Dallas. "I've made reservations at the World Trade Center."

He nodded and pulled away from the curb.

"Not bad," Marjory murmured more quietly to Paige, tossing her head toward Dallas.

Paige simply smiled. "So we're doing it up big tonight?"

"I figured I had to do something super after what I put you through today. Do you hate me?"

"I have to admit that there have been moments . . ."

"Tell me. I want to hear everything."

Paige began to detail her day. Marjory interrupted her regularly to ask questions, trying to read between the lines of the gallery owners' chatter. They reached their destination before Paige had even finished telling of the morning's appointments.

Dallas dutifully opened the door and helped each woman out in turn. His hand was just releasing Paige's—reluctantly?—when Marjory spoke.

"Give us several hours. We should be fortified by then." She moved forward with her customary confidence.

Paige lingered for a minute to look up at Dallas. "You'll get something to eat?" she asked in a whisper.

His lips twitched. "Beer and a sandwich sound mighty good. Not quite your champagne and caviar, but it'll do."

"I feel guilty."

"Nonsense." His hand slipped up her back and he gave her a gentle nudge forward. "Go on, and enjoy yourself. You deserve it."

She was about to argue that he did too when she saw that Marjory had stopped and was waiting for her. "Thanks," she murmured with a shy smile, then trotted ahead. Marjory promptly slipped an arm through the crook of her elbow and propelled her on.

"What was *that* all about?"

"What?"

"Soft whispers to your chauffeur."

Paige was grateful that the revolving door took them momentarily apart. By the time they were together again inside the building, she had her composure intact. "He's a nice guy."

"I'm glad of that. When the agency called this morning to say that Felix wouldn't be driving you, I was a little worried. They assured me that this fellow was capable."

"Capable ... and patient." Among other things. "If you and I found the heat to be oppressive today, think of what he must have felt."

"That's his job. He's paid well."

"Still ..."

They stood at all the elevator bank, waiting for a car to arrive to whisk them effortlessly to the one-hundred-and-seventh floor. Marjory eyed her cautiously. "Am I really seeing what I'm seeing?"

Paige schooled her expression to one of blankness. "What?"

"If I didn't know better, I'd think you like the guy."

"I told you. He's nice."

"No. I mean, *like* the guy. As in *being soft on*." She enunciated each word.

Paige's poise held. "Margie, he's my *driver*."

"He's also gorgeous. You didn't notice?"

"He is pleasant to look at."

"Aha! We're getting somewhere."

"Now, just a minute." Paige feigned annoyance. "I don't think I like what you're suggesting."

"I'm suggesting that every little admission is a small victory with you. Honestly, Paige. You're a woman. I know you to be warm and giving. But for some reason you insist on sublimating."

The elevator arrived and their discussion was momentarily curtailed as others entered the car. Paige didn't forget Marjory's comment, though. She felt strangely annoyed. It wasn't until they'd been seated at a table with a spectacular view of the city that she was able to pursue it.

"Explain how you think I sublimate."

"You pour your passion into your work, leaving none for the male of our species. Do you have something against men?"

Paige might have been further annoyed had it not been for Marjory's gentle tone. "Of course not."

"Then why do you avoid them? Really. There were at least a dozen eligible bachelors at the party last night, but you didn't notice one. I suppose it's none of my business, and you could tell me to shut up. But I care about you, Paige. You'd make someone a wonderful, loving wife."

Paige simply smiled with a return of her character-istic serenity. "Maybe. Someday. For now I'm just happy sculpting."

"Then you haven't ruled it out?"

"Marriage? Of course not. Come the day I meet the right man, I'll get married. I'm young. There's no rush."

Her utter composure told Marjory that it would be pointless to argue. Taking a deep breath, followed by a long sip of the martini the waiter had just delivered, Marjory returned the conversation to business.

By the time the elevator carried them back down to the ground floor, Paige had grown strangely edgy. She was tired, anxious to return to the limousine that had come to represent a haven of sorts. As always, the sight of Dallas waiting beside the car gave her a burst of en-ergy.

Since Marjory's apartment was in the East Village not far from the World Trade Center, it made sense to drop her first. The two women wouldn't be seeing each other again before Paige left the following noontime for home. Warm hugs punctuated their parting.

"You'll call me when you get home and let me know how it went with Groeffling?" Marjory demanded.

"I will. Thanks for everything, Margie. You've done a super job."

"Have to earn my commission, don't I?" Margie teased with a final squeeze before slipping from the car and waving as it started off.

Paige's thoughts had nothing to do with either the man she'd be meeting the next morning or her agent's commission as Dallas headed the limousine uptown. Her thoughts were on Dallas himself. She wanted to ask if he'd gotten his beer and sandwich but found herself tongue-tied. She wondered where he'd go after he dropped her off, who he'd be driving tomorrow, whether he affected all of his female charges this way.

His head, formally capped, was a dark silhouette. She would have given far more than a penny for his thoughts at that moment, but he seemed as disinclined to speak as she.

As Twenty-third Street became Thirty-fourth, then Forty-fifth, she felt a gnawing tension in her body that grew and spread until it radiated around her. Through a sprinkling of traffic the limousine cruised up Sixth Avenue to Central Park, turned east, then north again. All too soon it approached the Seventies, where her borrowed town house stood.

When Dallas turned onto her street, she shifted in her seat. She wanted something . . . didn't dare put it into words . . . felt a curiosity, a heat. . . .

Pulling the car into a parking space, he stilled the engine, then sat for just a moment while Paige held her breath. When he slowly opened his door and climbed out, she took her lower lip between her teeth. Tightly clutching her purse, she waited while he opened her door. If his hand closed more tightly than usual around hers, she attributed it to her imagination. No way, though, was she imagining the quickness of her own breath or the jumping of her stomach. Those things were too real, as was the fact that he didn't release her hand as they walked slowly toward the steps.

The glow from the streetlights dimmed as they descended the steps. When they stood in the small hollow before her front door, Paige slipped her hand from his so that she could reach into her purse for the key. Head bent, she closed her fingers around the hard metal and faltered. She wanted to say something, do something. . . .

A strong forefinger touched her skin, curving under her chin to very gently raise her head. Dallas was looking at her, his tall, sturdy form a mere breath away. She couldn't make out his expression, but his touch bore the unmistakable tension she thought had been hers alone. When he lowered his head she didn't move.

His lips brushed hers lightly once, then again. She knew he was giving her time to demur, to refuse him, to put him in his place. She could do nothing, though, but stand before him, entranced by the pleasure of his touch. Her eyes closed; she floated. He was slow, so slow, whispering the faintest of kisses against her lips until they opened with a will of their own in a soft blend of curiosity and desire.

Only then did he deepen the kiss. Only then did Paige learn what a real kiss was. It was warm. It was delicious. It was a moist caress that seared a fiery path through her bloodstream. It was increasingly hungry, caused increasing hunger. It was exciting, powerful and, in its way, frightening.

Stunned by the intensity of the pleasure she felt, she pulled back to look up at him. The shadows kept his expression a mystery, but the city sounds couldn't muffle the faint unevenness of his breathing.

"Have you got your key?" he murmured hoarsely. Nodding, she pulled it from her purse. He took it, turned it in the lock and pushed the door open.

Paige continued to study the dim outline of his features, half-afraid to believe that a man could make her feel so…so feminine. Not *a* man. *This* man. One she'd known for less than a day, one who was a virtual stranger to her by every reasonable measure. He was her driver… *her driver*. But it didn't matter. Nothing mattered but that he seemed to have the key to unlock feelings in her she'd feared had been frozen.

Turning to her now, he slid his fingers to the back of her neck and caressed the line of her jaw with his thumb. Its pad was faintly abrasive, broadcasting masculinity in the gentlest of ways. When he kissed her this time, her lips were open and waiting.

She had never known such delight; there was no way she could possibly turn from it. Instinct guided her…or was it Dallas himself? She only knew that what was happening, the response she felt and gave, was the most natural, the most exhilarating thing she'd ever experienced. Her lips yielded to his, then demanded in turn. Even her tongue found new purpose as it cavorted with his.

A shudder passed through Dallas and he raised his head. "Should I come in?" he asked, a definite thickness in his voice.

A shock of excitement ricocheted through her body at his words, his tone. She couldn't speak, simply nodded.

"Are you sure?"

Again she nodded. She held no illusions. Dallas wanted nothing more than what she wanted—a few moments' pleasure. The difference was that while this was surely nothing new to him, it was new to her. She wanted to know where the inner heat she felt would lead. If the night ended in failure, she had nothing to lose. She'd be leaving tomorrow, would never see Dallas again. If, on the other hand, the night ended in the ecstasy she'd only heard about, she'd have memories and the certain knowledge that she was a woman in every sense of the word. If that proved to be the case, Dallas would have no idea of the true service he'd performed this day.

Slipping his arm around her back, he guided her into the apartment and kicked the door shut. Then he turned her to him and, taking her face in his large hands, kissed her deeply. Every recess of her mouth was touched and explored. Her knees shook so wildly that she might have fallen had she not wound her arms around his neck. But there was discovery in that, too.

His shoulders felt as broad, as strong as they looked. His neck was warm, firmly corded. The hair at his nape was crisp, then soft and exquisitely enticing to her touch.

Releasing her face, he tossed his hat to the sofa and, wrapping his arms around her back, crushed her to him. Feeling his full strength for the first time, she might have been intimidated had it not been for the thrill of excitement the nearness brought.

His arms loosened and he ran his hands up and down her back. His head dipped. He buried his face against her neck while he gently eased off her jacket and dropped it to the side. When his hands moved on her again, the silk of her blouse was a sensual conduit. His fingers traced her spine, then spread around her middle, thumbs paving the way, burning her as they inched up her ribs.

She felt the swelling of her breasts moments before he covered them, and couldn't stifle the gasp that slipped from her lips when his fingers shaped her fullness and kneaded gently.

"Shh," he soothed, catching her lips with his as his thumbs zeroed in on the tight buds straining against the fabric. Back and forth he stroked. Paige had to gasp for breath. Her entire body seemed on fire, as though her veins were wicks carrying a spark from the spots he touched to her every extremity. She hadn't dreamed it could be like this, so flagrant, so all-consuming. She hadn't *dared* dream. But now she knew. And she wanted more. More of this phenomenal rapture that Dallas's touch inspired.

His breathing was as ragged as hers when he dragged his mouth away. Forehead resting against hers, he worked carefully at the buttons of her blouse. She wasn't sure if she could breathe, so great was the sense of anticipation, of excitement, of apprehension. She waited for something within her to still, to die, but nothing did. When her blouse lay completely open and his hands smoothed the silk from her shoulders, she felt more inflamed than ever.

The feeling only intensified when he began to caress her bare flesh. Her neck, her back, her ribs—every inch was covered in turn by his seeking hands. Her mouth opened widely beneath his, welcoming him with an abandon that might have stunned her had she been aware of it. But she only knew that what she felt was right and good and devastatingly healthy.

Within minutes he'd slipped his fingers beneath the thin straps of her teddy and eased them down her arms, pushing the fabric and her skirt low on her hips, leaving her torso bare to his gaze. The only light in the room was that which filtered in from the street through the gauzy drapes. It was enough. He held her back for a minute to admire what he'd uncovered, but the discovery was largely Paige's. She should have been shy at his blatant study of her nakedness; no man had ever examined her with quite such thoroughness. But what she felt was pride and hunger. She stood still as long as she could.

"Touch me," she whispered. Even her voice sounded foreign, its husky tone new to her ears but fully in keeping with the moment. "Please?"

He needed no more encouragement. His hands were warm against her flesh, exploring her curves with barely restrained eagerness. "You're very beautiful," he rasped, his fingers less steady than they'd been before.

Paige grasped his shoulders for support, not releasing them even when he knelt to free the rest of her body from the confines that seemed suddenly so restrictive. Skirt, teddy, nylons—each was tossed aside. When she was completely naked, he sat back on his heels, hands curved behind her thighs, to look at her again. She couldn't believe how her arousal was fueled by his gaze alone, but it was. Another discovery. She half wanted to call it off at this point if only to always remember the divine sensation of being worshiped in all her naked glory by a man. For he did worship her. His eyes, his expression, his subservient stance—she felt desirable, precious, powerful in her way.

But it wasn't enough. She grew conscious of the tight knot that had formed low in her belly and knew that, however glorious the moment was, there was still more to discover. She was on a voyage with a stranger and she was loving every minute of it.

Dallas swallowed audibly, then inched his hands slowly down her legs. He circled her ankles and began to climb back over her shins, but his gaze moved faster, coming to rest at the dark apex of her thighs. His hands reached her knees, which began to wobble with embarrassing instability. The message wasn't lost on him. With an abrupt glance at her face, as though he'd momentarily forgotten that part of her, he stood and began to quickly shed his clothes.

Paige watched, mesmerized, as each span of flesh was revealed. With the dispensing of his jacket, tie and shirt, she saw that his chest was firm, lightly haired in an erotic pattern that channeled her eyes to the belt he was unbuckling. He released the fastening of his trousers, lowered his zipper, thrust everything from his hips as he stepped out of his shoes. Then he was before her, as naked and aroused as she, and once again she was awed by the excitement of merely looking.

But Dallas had passed that point. He swept her into his arms and pressed her willing flesh to his. Chest to chest, belly to belly, thigh to thigh, they reveled in the intimate contact. Paige moaned. Dallas sighed. Winding their arms around the other's back, each held tightly as if to preserve that which could be so fleeting.

Then Paige was being lowered to the plush carpet and Dallas was looming over her. He kissed her, stroked her with a fever that might have been contagious had she not already been thoroughly afflicted. Foreplay was unnecessary; the day itself had been one long, taunting session. She was ready to explode even as she felt his first prodding touch. Her only thought of caution was one of a most practical nature.

"Dallas," she whispered urgently, "I don't...I haven't got anything..."

Arms trembling, he paused on the brink of penetration. "Oh, God."

"I'm sorry. I'm sorry. But I didn't plan..."

"Shh." He kissed her lightly and began to ease himself away.

Paige was suddenly frantic, imagining that her one chance at ultimate glory was being denied her by her own practicality. She clutched at his shoulders, willing him back. "It's okay...I'll take the chance...I think it's safe...."

"Shh, love. I have something." Sitting on his heels, still framed by her legs, he reached for his pants, rummaged in a pocket, found a condom and applied it. Then, as though hypnotized by the sight of her open and waiting for him, he lingered for a minute. Slipping his hands up her legs, he touched her gently, rotating his thumbs in ever-encroaching circles that revealed quite plainly her readiness for him.

"Please! Now!" she cried.

Surging forward, he propped his hands beneath her arms, bowed his back and thrust upward, bringing Paige such abrupt bliss that she feared she'd die of delight. She felt filled and fulfilled, but only until he began to move more steadily; then her desire left one plane and moved on to the next. A look of wonder gave a glow to her features. She was as astonished by her own sexuality as she was by the myriad ecstatic sensations the male form could generate. The excitement compounded itself, leaving her little control. Swept up in a dizzying twister of passion, she whirled round and round, higher and higher until, arching her back, she lay suspended for a long, pulsing moment before finally exploding into a series of rapturous spasms that left her gasping for air, clinging to Dallas, whispering his name in awe.

With the slow return of consciousness, she realized that he was still inside her, as hard and full as ever. She opened her eyes to find him smiling gently above her.

"You haven't . . ."

"I haven't come. I know. I was sidetracked watching you. That was something to behold."

She squeezed her eyes shut and turned her face aside with a moan. But Dallas's lips were sprinkling warm kisses on her cheek, then her nose and mouth.

"Don't be embarrassed," he breathed, his voice exquisitely gentle in its rough way. "You have no idea how arousing it is for a man to witness the pleasure he brings a woman. I had no idea, for that matter. So by rights I'm the one who should be embarrassed. I didn't know. It makes it all that much more wonderful. Don't you see?"

With a moment's thought, she did see. Further, she saw that he'd said what she needed to hear. She wasn't quite prepared for his next words, though, or for the twinkle in his eye that even the room's dimness couldn't hide.

"Besides, it makes this next part that much more of a challenge."

"A challenge?" she whispered.

"Uh-huh. Now I want to see if I can make it happen again."

"Oh, Dallas . . . I don't know . . . I feel . . ."

"Spent? That's why we're resting right now. You'll get your second wind. Just watch."

She hadn't expected the first wind and was still marveling at the incomparable joy of it. Second wind? If it never came, she'd still be in heaven. She'd done it! There was nothing wrong with her after all! To hell with Tyler and his inept fumblings so many years ago! To hell with all those who'd called her an ice maiden!

"I want to please you, Dallas," she whispered. "Tell me what to do."

"You do please me. You don't need instruction."

"But I want you to feel what I felt. I want to see it, too." She tightened herself around him and found, to her amazement, that she wasn't as drained as she'd thought. The feel of him deep inside her sent reborn tingles through her veins. When he slowly withdrew, then returned once again, she gasped in surprise.

"Feel good?"

His smugness was merited. "Oh, yes," she breathed.

He began to move steadily, then with increasing speed. She felt his arms tremble. Her wandering hands charted the tightening of his body. As the fire grew hotter, he closed his eyes, but she saw nothing beyond that, since her own eyes had closed under the force of renewed passion.

This time they climbed together, gasping in turn, kissing wildly until they needed every breath to surge with the growing delirium.

Moments before she reattained that newly discovered precipice, she cried his name. "Dallas!"

"Jesse," he panted hoarsely. "My . . . first name . . . is Jesse."

She never had a chance to say it. When he gave a deep moan and thrust a final time, wave after wave of ecstasy burst upon her, perfectly coinciding with the thunderous climax that shook his large frame.

It seemed an eternity before either of them could think, much less breathe. Dallas collapsed over her, then slid his slick body to the side. He left a limp arm draped across her waist, a long leg lying lethargically between hers. He pressed his lips to her bare shoulder and left them there, as though he had neither the strength nor the wish to move away.

Paige felt weak, totally drained. She was also unbelievably satisfied. Eyes closed, she dropped her head to rest against Dallas's hair. Her lips curved into a broad smile. Without intending to, she fell asleep.

Several hours later Dallas awakened her with a light kiss. She opened her eyes slowly. Only after a moment's disorientation did she remember where she was, who she was with, what they'd done together. Then, helplessly, her lips split into that same broad smile.

"You seem pleased with yourself."

He should only know, she thought. Very softly, she said, "I am."

"Do I take it everything was . . . satisfactory?"

Her eyes met his then and, rather than finding a smug expression on his face, she saw a glimmer of unsureness. "It was," she assured him quickly.

"No second thoughts? No regrets? After all, I am your . . . chauffeur."

"Are all chauffeurs such wonderful lovers?"

"I don't know. I've never made love to a chauffeur, myself."

His unsureness seemed to have eased. Tipping his head, he began to nibble on her ear. The moisture of his touch was infinitely pleasing. She slid her fingers into his hair, delighting in the vitality of the sandy shock.

His voice was muffled against the lobe of her ear when he spoke. "Do you do this often?"

"Nope."

"You seemed . . . stunned."

She knew exactly what he was referring to. It had nothing to do with his being a chauffeur and everything to do with the pleasure she'd felt. "I was."

"Why?"

"I . . . it was very strong."

"You've never felt it quite that way before?"

She hesitated for a minute, then whispered, "No."

Dallas appeared to be more than content with her simple answer. A low growl emerged from his throat, his breath tingling her shoulder bone, to which his lips had moved. He seemed intent on exploring and tasting, something neither of them had had time or patience for earlier.

Paige quickly discovered the pleasure of this, too. His mouth moved in leisurely progression, leaving no inch of her untouched. At times she was embarrassed, but her rising ardor quickly overcame that emotion—that, and the lilting words of encouragement and praise that Dallas lavished on her throughout his journey. If the heat built slowly, it was no less searing when he finally eased into her. And the pleasure she found was, if anything, all the more intense for the buildup.

It was a cycle that repeated itself throughout the night. They made love, slept, then woke up and made love again. For Paige, one discovery followed another. She learned ways to make love she'd never imagined, learned that her own participation, indeed, her initiative, was not only desirable to Dallas but infinitely rewarding to herself. At some point, he carried her upstairs to the cushioning softness of the bed, where, remarkably, their tired bodies found new strength.

The last thought she had when she drifted back to sleep shortly before dawn was that she would never, never forget the night that had been.

It was a good thing. When her alarm wrenched her from a blissfully deep sleep at nine, she was alone.

3

PAIGE SMILED. She remembered more, and her smile widened. With a feline stretch, she grew aware of a myriad unfamiliar muscles and chuckled softly. She took a deep breath and turned onto her side, facing that half of the bed where her lover had lain.

Dallas. What a wonderful man. He'd been gently forceful, tenderly fierce. Feeling irrepressibly buoyant, she laughed aloud, threw back the sheet that covered her and bounded from bed. She'd spent the night in the arms of her chauffeur. In theory, it was deliciously scandalous, decidedly decadent. In reality, it was the most wonderful thing that had ever happened to her.

Knowing that she was to be picked up at ten for her last appointment of the trip, she showered, dressed, packed her bag and set it neatly by the front door, then made herself a cup of coffee. All the while her thoughts were on the night that had been. She had no regrets — she'd done what she'd wanted to do. Now she could return to her house by the sea, to the skylit studio she loved so much and to her work, knowing for the first time in her life that she was complete. Whether or not she ever again found the passion to which Dallas had introduced her, she would be always grateful for the night now past. Because of it she could rest assured that, sexually, she was lacking in no way, shape or form. With this knowledge, she felt she could bring to her work an even greater sensitivity. She couldn't wait to sculpt again.

Promptly at ten the doorbell rang. Its peal spawned a strange inkling of self-doubt. She assumed that Felix would be back today. But if he wasn't? If it was Dallas at the door? How would she act? How would he?

Having already washed her coffee cup and checked that there was no lingering trace of her presence in the borrowed town house, she headed for the window. Yes, that was the limousine outside. But who had driven it here?

Stilling the tiny butterflies that flitted through her stomach, she opened the door and found—to her relief, or disappointment?—that Felix had indeed returned.

"Good morning, Miss Mattheson," the small and very proper chauffeur said. "How are you today?"

"Just fine, Felix." She gave a last, perhaps wistful glance around the room, then sighed. "I do believe I'm ready."

Having already lifted her suitcase, Felix stood aside for her to pass, then closed the door firmly. If Paige heard the solid thud as symbolic of the end of a very brief, very brilliant moment in her life, she was quickly consoled by the knowledge she'd attained from it. She felt as though she were a different woman from the one who had left Marblehead three days before. And, she reasoned, it was probably better that she not see Dallas again. After all, he had his life—whatever it was—and she had hers.

She wasn't sure how many times she repeated that litany during the drive to her appointment, or how often she thought of it during the meeting itself. She knew that her mind was not on the rotund gallery keeper before her, or on the handful of collectors he'd invited for midmorning tea. By the time she finally emerged into the city heat once more, her thoughts were fully directed toward home.

That was before she caught sight of Dallas pushing off from the side of the limousine to stand straight and tall, awaiting her.

Ignoring a sudden weakness in her knees, she walked steadily forward. He touched the visor of his cap in a mute greeting, only the searing blue of his eyes bearing hint that there'd ever been anything other than total formality between them.

She came to a halt at the car door that he'd opened and gave a shy smile. "I...didn't expect you." Her body hadn't either, but that didn't stop the leaping and bounding that had already commenced therein. Once again she marveled at the effect the simple sight of this man had on her, though now there was far more than his looks to stimulate her. There were memories, mental images of naked bodies enmeshed with each other, of hands and lips and tongues exploring and caressing, of backs arching, hips thrusting.

"I didn't expect me either," Dallas murmured soberly.

For an instant Paige feared he'd been pressed into a service he clearly didn't want. Her stomach knotted. "I'm sorry," she whispered, then ducked her head and slid into the limousine.

Dallas leaned in after her. "I'm not. That wasn't what I meant."

"It's all right." She forced a smile. "It'll be pretty boring for you driving all the way to Marblehead and back. I don't blame you." She frowned. "Uh, unless I've misunderstood. Felix was to drive me home. Where is he?"

"Back at the agency. I'll be driving you home."

After having reconciled herself to never seeing him again, she wasn't sure how she felt about the change in plans. With the firm shutting of her door and Dallas's sliding into the driver's seat, though, it appeared that she had no choice.

Settling back, she concentrated on the buildings they passed, on the bustle of city life she was leaving at last. Only three days she'd been here, yet it seemed longer. So much had happened—so much of it centering around the man in front of her.

Quite helplessly, she smiled. She felt good, better and better as they sped along the East River then crossed over the Triborough Bridge. She was going home with her memories, an even brighter outlook on life, *and* the man who had made it all possible.

Dallas's feelings were far more mixed. Time and again he asked himself what he was up to. He'd won his bet, though he hadn't thought to call Ben with the news. By the time he'd returned to the brownstone he owned, a short two blocks from where he'd left Paige sleeping so blissfully, he'd been so confused that he'd been able to do nothing but shower and shave, then sit in a chair wondering what in the devil to do next.

He'd been right—Paige Mattheson was passionate to the core. Innocent and without guile, she'd been an incredible lover. Far from leaving him cold, as every other woman in recent memory had done, she'd left him aching for more. He'd taken her again and again, finding joys in lovemaking that he, for all his experience, had never known before.

He should have left it at that. But he couldn't. He'd picked up the phone no less than three times before he'd finally done what he knew he had to do. He had to see Paige again, learn where she lived, spend just that little bit more time with her. There was something about her that went far beyond one night's interest and, much as he resented it, he was helpless to deny his fascination.

The agency had been as agreeable in granting his request that he drive Paige home today as it had been when he'd wangled his way into driving her around the city. The fact that the owner of the agency was an old acquaintance of his hadn't hurt. Neither had the fact that Jesse Dallas was a respected member of the media community, perhaps not as flashy or powerful as some, but respected nonetheless.

What Jesse didn't understand was why he was chasing after a woman this way. He never chased women. He used them, discarded them. So why was he here, masquerading as a chauffeur, no less? And what did he expect was going to happen when they finally arrived in Marblehead at the seaside home that this woman loved so much?

A dry smile toyed at the corners of his mouth. Oh, he knew what he wanted to happen. Even now he felt a telltale tightening in his groin. Man, was he sore! He'd worked his body—or had it worked him?—in inspiring and inspired ways last night. *She* had done that to him. Paige Mattheson. Frigid? Not by a long shot! He didn't know about her, but aches and all, he was ready for another go-round right now.

Daring a glance in the rearview mirror, he saw that her head lay against the back of the seat. Her eyes were closed. She wore a serene expression that was almost disturbing in its beauty. He wondered if she was thinking of their lovemaking, too, but didn't have the courage to ask. Didn't have the courage? Since when had he not had the courage to speak his mind before a woman? Bastard, many had called him when he'd been his usual blunt self. Perhaps he was a bastard. Certainly he was a loner, a man who prized his independence. He had a good job, one that demanded his every waking hour from the moment he began an assignment to its completion.

Fortunately he was on R and R right now. Otherwise he'd never have been able to come in pursuit of Paige this way.

He winced at his own choice of words. And the cycle of equivocation began again.

For better than two hours they drove in relative silence. They were approaching Hartford, their halfway point, when at last Dallas spoke. "Hungry?"

Paige raised her head and looked around. She'd been so buried in her own thoughts that she hadn't charted the progress of the car as she might otherwise have done. "A little," she answered quietly.

"There's a super place at the Civic Center. Continental-type food. Interested?"

"Very." In point of fact, hunger was secondary. She'd been wondering if Dallas was ever going to talk to her again. Lunch at a continental-type restaurant in the Civic Center sounded promising.

Obviously familiar with the city, Dallas knew just which exit to take, which way to turn after that. Paige wasn't at all surprised when, rather than dropping her at the front of the restaurant as Felix might have done, he drove into the huge parking garage adjacent to the center and parked.

She didn't think of Dallas as her chauffeur. When he tossed his cap onto the seat and helped her out, he was her escort. Her tall, handsome, breathtakingly sexy escort. When he took her hand in his, it seemed the most natural thing in the world. Without words he confirmed that the night before had been no dream, as she'd half begun to wonder during the silent drive north.

He handled himself smoothly, speaking in quiet tones to the maître d', gesturing toward the table he wanted, a quiet one by a large potted palm. By the time they'd been seated, Paige was feeling surprisingly happy, if vaguely shy. She waited for him to speak to her, which he did only after he'd ordered a bottle of what she recognized to be a very fine white wine. It occurred to her that the agency might not be thrilled.

"This is on me," he said quietly, finding it a matter of pride that she know he was no parasite. Despite what he'd so blithely said when she'd offered to pay for their cold drinks yesterday, he refused to bill the agency for anything, least of all his time. Even beyond the issue of pride, he felt less . . . devious doing it this way.

"I was wondering," she answered as softly, a hint of teasing in the eyes he saw now to be the prettiest of jade. He wondered why he hadn't noticed them before, realized he'd been distracted by...other aspects of the intriguing woman before him.

For long moments he simply stared at those eyes, trying to understand why they fascinated him so. They were shy without being coy, warm without being suggestive. He found himself decidedly content staring into their depths. It was this very contentment that struck a note of annoyance in him.

"How do you feel?" he asked.

"Fine."

"No...regrets the morning after?"

"It's the afternoon." The shyness she'd felt was slowly burning off, as a fog beneath the sun, leaving a light-heartedness shining from her face. He was the one who was awkward, she realized. The knowledge made him that much more endearing.

"You know what I mean."

"Yes. And no, I have no regrets." Her soft smile supported her claim.

"Are you surprised that I'm here?"

"A little. I didn't expect to see you again."

"Did you want to?"

"I wasn't sure."

If he had hoped to unsettle her with his bluntness, he was failing badly. Despite her words, she seemed very sure of herself. And she seemed unbothered by the arrogance that he knew shadowed his questions.

"What were you thinking?" he prodded, driven by ego as much as by anything else.

"I was thinking that even if I never saw you again, I'd remember last night. It was very special."

"Glad to hear it. You shouldn't have hoped I'd come today, though. I'm unreliable in that way."

"I wasn't hoping. Just wondering."

"You weren't hoping? Not just a little?"

She looked down and stifled a grin. "I think I'm denting your armor."

"Of course not. Well, maybe a little. Every man likes to think that once he's made a woman his, she can't wait to see him again."

Raising her head, she looked at him. Her gaze held if not smugness then at least full command of the moment. "Is that what you did . . . made me yours?"

His cheeks burned. And he thought *he* was direct!

"Well, euphemistically speaking, I suppose. Some men feel possessive toward the woman they've made love to."

"Do you?"

"No. I don't believe in ties like that."

"You've got nothing to fear from me," she said.

Her utter sincerity set him back again. For an instant he wondered if perhaps Ben had been right. There was passion, and there was passion. Paige now seemed so calm, so self-assured that he had to force himself to remember how she'd been last night. "You don't believe in ties?"

"I don't need to belong to someone—" She raised her eyes and stopped speaking when the waiter brought their wine. He made ceremony of uncorking it, poured a sample for Dallas to taste, then, with his approval, filled their glasses. When Dallas promptly ordered for both himself and Paige, she indulged him. She was secure enough of her individuality not to be threatened by his gesture of dominance.

"A toast," he said, lifting his glass as soon as the waiter had gone. "To us."

Looking deep into his eyes, Paige nodded once, then took a sip of her wine. How did one respond to such a toast? To agree was to suggest some future relationship, yet she held no pretense on that score. To disagree, on the other hand, was rude. And perhaps a lie. Though she had no designs on Dallas's future, she couldn't rule out the possibility that they might see each other from time to time.

"You were saying?" he drawled, setting down his glass, placing his forearms on the table and interlacing his fingers.

Though, as always, Paige was affected by his nearness, she was undaunted by his taunting tone. "I was saying," she resumed on the same soft note, "that I like my life as it is. I enjoy living by myself. I enjoy my independence."

"But you enjoyed last night, didn't you?"

"I told you, I did. That doesn't mean that I need it tonight. I'm not a hanger-on, Dallas—"

"Jesse," he whispered, then paused. "Say it."

His whisper stirred all those things in her that she'd felt the day before. Where his curtness couldn't stir her, his softness did.

"Jesse," she whispered back, then lowered her eyes self-consciously and laughed. "I think I'll always think of you as Dallas. Jesse feels . . . strange."

"Strange as in personal? Intimate? Will you always think of me as your chauffeur?"

"But I don't," she argued quickly, knowing it was true. Though she'd said the words in her mind, even voiced them to Marjory, she'd never in her heart believed them, not in the truest of senses, certainly not by way of condescension. To her, Dallas's occupation had been incidental, and more than a little mystifying, given his obvious social grace. Sitting across from her as he was, wearing his tailored navy suit and an air of thorough comfort in as high-priced a restaurant as this was, he might have been a lawyer or a stockbroker or a playboy who'd inherited millions. Maybe that was it, she mused. Maybe he worked as a chauffeur for kicks. But kicks . . . suffering boredom and the heat as he'd done yesterday? Of course, the results had been well worth his while. Perhaps he'd simply devised a new way to combat the singles' scene, guaranteeing himself wealthy women, to boot. *There* was a thought that *did* bother her. It made her feel used. Dirty.

"Do you do this often?" she heard herself ask. The need to know was suddenly very great.

"Do what?"

"Pick up women this way?"

For the first time that afternoon, he seemed amused. "You mean, do I often seduce my passengers?" When she gave a hesitant nod, his smile broadened. "No. This was a first."

"Why did you do it?"

"That's a naive question." Even as he said it, he felt the slightest bit guilty. For one thing, there was the matter of the deception he practiced. For another, there was the bet he'd made with Ben. But neither of those facts touched at the root of the matter. "The attraction was there from the beginning," he said more quietly.

"Did it . . . bother you?"

"Should it have?"

She shrugged, not quite sure what she was getting at, herself. "I don't know."

"Look, Paige," he offered, feeling a sudden need to put her at ease. "The attraction I feel for you is as natural as that which you feel for me. There's nothing wrong with it, and I refuse to apologize. No, I don't make a practice of picking up women that way, but I'm not sorry things happened as they did. You're a very special lover."

It was Paige's turn to blush then, which she did with uncommon innocence. But she was pleased. She'd never dared think that any man might call her what Dallas just had. It boggled her mind.

"That's pretty," he murmured, brushing the back of his fingers against her cheek.

"What is?" she whispered.

"Your blush. I couldn't see it last night in the dark. Were you blushing then, too?"

Her color deepened all the more. When he was like this, his voice so gentle and gravelly, her insides tickled. "At times."

"Surely there've been other men."

"Obviously."

"Many?"

"One."

"Only one?" He couldn't curb his surprise, though it helped explain the wonder he'd seen on her face at various times during the night. "Why is that, Paige? You're a beautiful woman. You obviously feel the right things at the right times."

"It wasn't always that way."

"What do you mean?"

She studied him with gentle eyes, abundantly aware of the intimacies they'd shared. One more seemed in order. She saw no point in being evasive, and she had nothing to be ashamed of now that she *knew*. "There was an artist a long time ago. We were both very young. He assumed I was frigid. I was never quite sure...until last night."

If Dallas's ego had been shaky, her words set it on firm ground. It was a heady thought—that he'd been able to draw from her what no other man had. "No wonder you look so pleased with yourself."

"I am." Here, with Dallas, she felt feminine through and through. It was a new image of herself. She rather liked it.

"Then—" Dallas frowned, trying to put the pieces of the puzzle together "—you've avoided men over the years out of fear?"

"Oh, no. I just wasn't interested." At the narrowing of his eyes, she came to her own defense. "I wasn't. Honestly. My life is very full, what with my work. It's not as if I've been aware of any great void. I'm not aware of any now, for that matter. Last night taught me something about myself, but it won't necessarily change the way I live."

"You don't want a husband . . . or children?"

"By all means. But there's no rush. Why are you looking at me that way? I'm not unusual in this day and age."

"You're unusual," Dallas stated, swirling the wine in his glass, then draining it. When he set the glass down, he looked her in the eye. "I'm still not sure I believe it. You have a kind of self-containment that's remarkable. I can't remember when I've met anyone as sure of herself."

"Oh, I have my moments of insecurity."

"When?"

"When I'm sculpting. Or rather, when I finish. I may love what I've done. After all, there's a little bit of myself in everything I do. Unfortunately, more often than not, I then have to send the piece to one gallery or another. It's like baring oneself to the world. I'm not all that secure until I hear from Margie that the piece has been well received."

"Aha! So you *do* care what they think of you?"

"Not of me. Of my work. I'd be less than human if I didn't."

"But you said you didn't care if you ever sold—"

"Selling is one thing, and I don't care about that. But—" she struggled for the words to express what she felt "—sculpting is creating. It's taking something ostensibly without form and shaping it into an object with meaning. If my meaning doesn't get across, I'm crushed."

"Has that ever happened?"

"Several times."

"What do you do then?"

She grinned. "I keep clay on hand. It's therapeutic. Several hours of slapping it on the bench, giving it shape then slapping it into a blob again usually does the trick."

"A little temper tantrum, eh?"

"You could say."

"And then you feel better?"

"*Then* I have the courage to call Margie back. She's great for consolation. By that time she's usually been able to shift the piece to another gallery. I suppose it must be like having a child. You pour sweat and tears into its rearing and send it off into the world only to find that it's found a niche that isn't right. Things like that can be remedied, though it's plenty painful until they are."

Dallas was shaking his head, sighing deeply. "You'd probably be devastated as a mother when another kid on the block called yours names."

"I'm sure I would be."

"And that doesn't discourage you from ever having children?"

He wasn't just making conversation. Paige sensed there was deep feeling in his words. She wondered where his streak of pessimism came from. For some reason she couldn't ask.

"I'm not discouraged. My work is basically strong. Often it's simply a question of finding the right home for it. I assume the same is true of children. You instill in them certain values, build certain strengths. If you've done it right, they find their place, regardless of what trials they may have getting there."

"Is that what happened to you?"

"No. I've been lucky. Life's been kind all along. But I've seen others who've gone through hard times. They survived." She was thinking, most specifically, of one of her brothers. She'd always viewed him as the most creative of the three Mattheson boys, yet somehow he'd been channeled into a mathematical career where his creativity stagnated. He'd moved from one high-tech corporation to another, and was increasingly miserable, until at last he'd thrown caution to the winds and had signed on to write computer programs for a fledgling software manufacturer. Though his income was nowhere near where it had been, he was finally happy.

"Tell me about yourself, Paige," Dallas asked softly.

"Isn't that what I've been doing?"

"No. I mean, about what you were like as a child. What your family's like. How you got to be so lucky."

The arrival of their lunch gave Paige several minutes to compose her thoughts. It was only after they'd sampled and approved their cold duck salads that she spoke.

"I grew up in Connecticut."

"Whereabouts?"

"Westport."

"Ahh. That says a lot."

She knew it did, which was why she usually didn't volunteer that particular bit of information. She wasn't sure why she had done so now, only she knew that something in Dallas's intense gaze wouldn't permit less than the full truth. "Yes. That's one of the ways in which I was lucky. My father was—is—a bank executive. We grew up—"

"We?"

"I have three older brothers." When Dallas nodded, she went on, "We grew up with many of the things that others never have. Not only material things, but good health . . . and love."

"Do your parents still live in Westport?" She nodded. "Are you close?"

"Very."

"Were they at the party the other night?"

"No. I didn't want them there." She pushed a cherry tomato around her plate. "I . . . shows like that are hard for me. I'd rather see my parents in more relaxed times."

"Hard for you? You looked totally in control." When her head came up and she eyed him strangely, Dallas realized his error. To her knowledge, he hadn't been at that party. "What I mean is that you always seem so cool and self-assured. I can't imagine your having trouble anywhere."

This time her gaze was lightly chiding. "You, more than anyone, should know better. If it hadn't been for you yesterday, I might never have made it."

"You'd have made it," he said gruffly, then softened his tone. "But it was fun, wasn't it?"

She smiled, shyly, and nodded. It *had* been fun—a picnic in the park, gentle conversation, a companion. Then, of course, there had been last night. The memory stirred her as she looked into the blue eyes sparkling before her. She felt lured, drawn in. Suddenly she wanted to reach out and touch him, those lean, faintly shadowed cheeks, that mouth. She took a deep breath, then let it out in a long, unsteady sigh, and finally smiled. "You are inspiring, Dallas. Has anyone ever told you that before?"

DALLAS REPEATED those words time and again in his mind during the rest of the drive. Not only the words, but their attendant expression. He'd been giving her his guaranteed-to-knock-'em-dead stare, and she'd simply absorbed it, taken a deep breath and smiled. The master was slipping, that's all there was to it. By rights she should have already invited him to spend the night.

But she hadn't. In fact, she seemed perfectly content with the notion that last night had happened and was done. He had to believe she still wanted him. There had been the unevenness of her breath, the faint tremor of the pulse at her neck.

But she was in control. Cool, firm control. And he? He wanted her more than ever. Perhaps it was the challenge that appealed to him. Yes, that was enough of an excuse to try to seduce her a second time. As soon as they reached her beachfront home, he'd simply take her in his arms and she'd melt. He knew it.

It would be too easy. Too quick. No, for Paige he'd have to come up with a more cunning approach. After all, where would the fun be otherwise?

THE JOKE WAS ON HIM. Sitting alone in the huge limousine, parked on the shoulder of the road, Dallas stared moodily across the water at the darkening horizon. He was as taut as a wire, as frustrated as if he'd been bound by one with no hope of escape. He'd miscalculated somewhere. Trying to understand what had happened, he reviewed the events of the hours now past.

After leaving the restaurant, they'd returned to the highway. Conversation had been intermittent and light.

Paige had been as calm, as self-possessed as ever, even more so as they'd neared her home. It had been as though she approached Shangri-la. She'd relaxed fully, kicking her shoes off and stretching out on the seat. When at last they'd left the highway, she'd rolled down her window and deeply breathed in the fresh sea air.

If he'd thought Paige beautiful before, he hadn't seen her on her home turf. She'd grown happier by the minute, almost as though she were a child seeing the ocean for the first time. Her cheeks pinkened. Her eyes brightened. When she'd reached up and pulled the pins from her hair, letting it fall gracefully behind her shoulders, she'd looked like that child . . . yet every bit a woman. He'd actually adjusted the rearview mirror to more easily see her. She'd been a vision.

He'd barely pulled the long limousine to a halt when she had her shoes back on and was out the door. She'd stood still then, shoulders back, head up to the breeze. She'd inhaled once, and again. Then, as if fortified by the most potent drug in the world, she'd turned to him with the most brilliant of smiles.

"Great, isn't it?" she'd said, but hadn't given him time to answer, for she'd run up the pebbled walk and entered the house before he'd barely climbed from the car.

After opening the trunk and removing her suitcase, he'd taken a minute to admire the home she loved. He had to admit that it was magnificent. Contemporary, and sprawling over its own minipeninsula, it combined fieldstone and shingle to create a distinctly natural effect. With a steep sloped roof, it backed onto the sea. Even before he entered the large open living room he'd guessed what he'd find. Glass facing the sea. Walls and walls of glass. Living room, dining room, kitchen, bedrooms—she'd given him the grand tour, enjoying every minute of it herself. Her pride had been boundless, most evident in the studio, which stood in one wing.

"Did you have it built yourself?" he'd asked, sensing that the house was her, through and through. It fit her perfectly.

"Oh, no. I lucked out here, too. The man who built it—an architect—was moving south. He'd put it on the market the very day I came looking. Houses go fast here, particularly ones overlooking the ocean."

How long they'd stood in that living room, staring out over the weathered deck toward the sea, Dallas didn't know. The waves had mesmerized him almost as much as they mesmerized Paige, who stood beside him. Almost, but not quite. He'd been aware of her every breath, of the way her lips curved into a dreamy smile, of the way her heart beat.

He'd taken her in his arms then and kissed her with every bit of the tenderness she inspired. And tenderness had yielded to hunger as he'd known it would. Her lips had been warm and moist, her body arching into his.

Only when he'd sensed her total surrender—when her hands had begun to roam his back in silent invitation, when her lips had begun to demand on their own—had he set her back.

"Take care," he'd whispered. Pressing a final kiss on her forehead, he'd turned and left.

She'd wanted him, just as he'd known she would. And unless she truly was hard as stone, she'd have plenty to think about that night. Unfortunately, so would Dallas. He hadn't counted on the toll his cleverness would take on his own body.

Climbing from the car, he walked around to lean against its hood and face the sea. The air was refreshing, its evening coolness some relief on his fevered skin. The rustle of the high grasses behind him soothed. The surf lulled. He could see why she'd been so anxious to return. What he didn't see was what *he* was going to do about the ache that lingered.

Then he stood straight and knew what he was going to do. He was going to drive straight back to New York, return the fool limousine, put in a random call to one of the names in his little black book and forget that Paige Mattheson existed.

Perhaps he'd even call Ben and gloat. After all, he'd won the bet, hadn't he?

AS IT TURNED OUT, the only thing he did that night was return the limousine. By the time he reached home, he was thoroughly exhausted. Wandering from room to room, he felt strange, displaced. He ran his finger along things as he ambled—the back of the long leather sofa in the living room, the thick oak banister leading upstairs, the bookshelves that lined both the bedroom and den on the second floor, the edge of the metal table in his workroom on the third. He stared distractedly at the two TV-monitors atop the table, then at the leader that fed film from one screen to the other. These were the tools of his trade. He knew them as intimately as he'd known any woman, and Lord knew he spent much more time with them.

Why, then, did he feel unsettled? By rights he should be very much at home and content. The Kem machine was his closest friend, the nearest thing he had to a long-standing mistress. Had he lost interest in her, too? Why was it she suddenly seemed so cold and unappealing? Was it simply that he wasn't working, that there was no film now flowing through the mazes connecting screen to screen?

Without even bothering to flip on his answering machine and find out if anyone had called, he retraced his steps to the bottom floor, poured himself a healthy glassful of Scotch and sagged down onto the sofa.

The next thing he knew, it was morning. Late morning. The empty glass lay on its side on the floor. His muscles were cramped from confinement on the sofa all night. Sitting up, he propped his elbows on spread knees and dropped his face into his hands. His head ached. His neck was stiff. He felt as he did when he worked round the clock on a tight deadline, except that this morning he had nothing to show for his time. Nothing whatsoever.

A glance at his watch told him it was nearly noon. Pushing himself from the sofa, he went into the kitchen, poured himself a cold glass of milk, then drank it slouched against the counter. A police siren screamed in the distance. Scowling, he wondered where it was headed, what it would find when it got there. Forced entry? Robbery? Perhaps a little murder? Depressing.

Setting the glass none too gently in the sink, he climbed to his third-floor workroom and turned on the answering machine to find that his agent had called the day before. Urgent, he'd said. With a sigh, Dallas dialed his number. The secretary put him right through.

"John?"

"It's about time you got back to me!"

"I just got the message." He was in no mood to argue. "What's up?"

"Wagner called. He wants you to edit the piece he did in Nicaragua."

"I didn't know he was doing anything in Nicaragua."

"Neither did he. It was pretty last minute. He didn't think he'd be able to get into the country. When the okay finally came, he grabbed cameras and crew and ran."

"Nice."

"Well? Will you do it?"

"No."

"Why not?"

"I'm on vacation."

"Come on, Jesse. This is a great opportunity. We're talking hot film."

"I'm on vacation."

"You're there, aren't you? How long could this take— a week, maybe two? So you'll take your vacation then."

"I want it now."

"The money's good."

"The money was good on the prison piece I just finished, which is why I don't need to work for a while."

"Hey, where's your ambition? Wagner's the best, and he wants *you*."

Dallas ran a hand through his already-disheveled hair and sighed. "Another time, okay, John?" he coaxed wearily. "I'm just not up for it now. It'd be far worse to take the job and do it poorly than to simply explain that the timing's not right. Wagner will understand. You'll handle it well. Diplomacy's your specialty."

"Hmph. Thanks to you I get plenty of practice. Sure you won't reconsider? It's a plum."

"I'm sure."

"Are you all right?"

"Sure."

"You sound down."

"Naw. Just tired. Nothing a few weeks' rest won't cure."

A few weeks' rest. He thought about it as he hung up the phone. He did need a few weeks' rest. And not here. The city was about as restful as an army of ants.

He could fly up to the Gaspé. The small inn he'd stayed at two years ago had been restful enough. Boring, but restful. Or out to the Rockies. Of course, there wouldn't be any skiing this time of year. The Caribbean? But it'd be hot as hell.

In that instant he knew that he might name a hundred spots and find something wrong with each. There was one spot, though, that interested him. It'd be cool and refreshing, what with the steady breeze off the ocean. It'd be interesting, doubtlessly stimulating. He could take his time, sate his curiosity, get her out from under his skin once and for all.

Without further deliberation, he trotted downstairs, shaved and showered, then pulled out his duffel bag and filled it with the clothes he'd need. His headache had miraculously eased, as had the stiffness of his limbs. In fact, he felt remarkably peppy.

Within the hour he was on his way north.

4

PARKING HIS CAR in the driveway of the rambling house, Dallas climbed out, stretched, breathed deeply of the salty air much as Paige had done when they'd arrived here nearly twenty-four hours before. It was late in the afternoon, still warm, though the breeze was welcome relief from the heat he'd left behind in the city.

He started up the front path, then changed his mind and veered off onto a smaller path that led around the house toward the sea. The roar of the surf lured him on. He passed low-growing shrubs and trees that miraculously withstood the coastal elements. At a low stone wall he stopped. Beyond him was a sloping hill of rock, beyond that the sea. For long moments he stared at it, feeling more refreshed by the minute.

Then he glanced up toward the deck extending high on his left and caught his breath. Paige stood there, so absorbed in her thoughts that she was oblivious to his presence.

It had been an odd day for her. She'd been up early, had walked the beach feeling strangely unsure as to what she wanted to do. She'd known what she *should* do; she should get to work on a stupendous piece, the first to send to one of the galleries she'd visited. She'd already sent thank-you notes—last night when she'd been unable to fall asleep—to those who'd hosted her.

But in the morning light she'd still felt restless, unable to settle down. Perhaps she needed a day to unwind, she'd told herself.

Then she'd spotted a stone on the beach. She'd picked it up, turned it in her hand, studied it, read its heart. And she'd known what she wanted to do. It was something personal, something she'd never sell. But working on it all day as she'd done, she felt more at peace than she had since . . . since Dallas had left.

Mesmerized, Dallas stared at her. She wore a red blouse, knotted at midriff, and white shorts. Her hair blew free in the breeze. Arms wrapped around her waist, she seemed in a world of her own, a world she shared with her house and the sea.

For the first time he stopped to consider that he was intruding. She was a woman of solitude. She might not want him here.

But his needs at that moment were too great to allow for his turning and leaving as he'd done yesterday. He had to see her. He had to hold her.

At his first movement toward the plank steps leading from ocean to deck, Paige looked around sharply. Heart racing, she watched Dallas swing himself from the low stone wall to a midway point on the stairs. He boldly loped the rest of the way, slowing only when he'd reached the deck, halting only when he stood before her.

He tried to judge her reaction by her expression. Round-eyed, she was startled, as obviously a woman would be who had suddenly and unexpectedly found a man making his way to her deck. She was unsure—the way she bit her lower lip attested to that. And she was vulnerable; it was written all over her face.

This vulnerability was something he hadn't seen in her before and it had a strange effect on him. Rather than sweeping her into his arms and promptly picking up where he'd left off the day before, he lifted a hand to her cheek and caressed her softness with his thumb. She seemed suddenly like porcelain, fragile, delicate, but not at all cold and untouchable. Rather, she inspired tenderness and a protectiveness that would have stunned him had he not been so entranced by the spell she cast.

"Hi," he breathed softly.

She smiled, still uncertain. She hadn't expected him, had assumed, after yesterday, that he'd gone for good. She didn't know what to expect now, only knew that, somewhere deep inside, she was pleased to see him.

He cleared his throat and cast a quick glance down at his shirt and jeans. "I, uh, I figured I'd better go home and change. A suit just isn't right for the ocean."

She laughed, a soft laugh that was half whisper, and lowered her eyes. His jeans were clean but worn, fitting his hips well. His shirt, neatly starched, was plaid, the top two buttons open. Arms bare below his short sleeves, his skin was firm, lightly haired, exuding warmth.

"You look fine now," she whispered, finding her breath in short supply.

"I feel better." He kept his thumb busy at her cheek while he gently spread his other fingers into her hair. "You looked so pretty standing here. A beautiful statue."

Her eyes met his then with a message that went beyond her words. "I'm no statue."

"I know," he murmured shakily, then lowered his head and opened his mouth over hers. His lips barely touched at first but coasted lightly as, eyes closed, he savored the fact that he was here again, at last. She seemed unreal, far too precious for him. He knew he should stop himself. He knew he should never have come. He'd only hurt her, as he'd so many women in the past. But none of those others lured him as Paige did with her self-assurance, her poise, the vulnerability that had seeped through her veneer for that very short time. He knew he should leave, but he couldn't. He needed her too badly.

Only when he felt her lips part beneath his did he kiss her fully, and even then it was with a care that was novel for him. She tasted warm and sweet, very special. And she returned his kiss with the same kind of care. There was a softness to her—her lips, her tongue, the moist inner recesses of her mouth—that branded her different, and he found himself trembling under the responsibility he'd taken upon himself.

He drew back to find that her eyes were closed. She seemed in a trance, her expression dreamlike. He traced her lips with the tip of his tongue. When her own tongue crept out to meet it, he gasped. Hugging her fully to him, he buried his face in her hair.

"Paige . . . Paige . . ." he rasped, knowing that, for all the gentleness she inspired, he had to have her now. His hands roamed steadily and widely, exploring her shoulders, her back, her hips and thighs before returning to her bottom and crushing her hips to his. "I need you, Paige. God help me, but I need you!"

She nodded against his shoulder, her hands clutching at the corded muscles of his back. She couldn't think beyond the moment, beyond the heavenly state of pleasure Dallas created. She was attuned to her body, and its every sense ached for him. Only now did she admit how disturbed she'd been last night when he'd kissed her so enticingly and then left. Sexual frustration was new to her; she wasn't sure she liked it.

But Dallas was here now, promising the same bliss he'd shown her that sultry night in New York. But she knew so little about him. Would he arouse her again, then leave before bringing her the fulfillment her body craved?

Hands on his shoulders, she held him back. "Dallas, don't start if ... if ..."

He read the fear in her eyes and it turned his insides to jelly. "I won't, love," he murmured, smoothing the hair back from her face. "I won't leave. Is that what's got you worried?" When she nodded, he brought her back into his embrace. His limbs trembled under the self-restraint he imposed. His breath was warm in her hair. "I'm sorry for last night. I was a bastard. If it's any consolation, I was in agony all the way to New York. I should have turned around before I'd ever reached the highway and come back, but I'm dumb sometimes. Really dumb." Holding her back, he framed her face with his hands. His voice was little more than a breath. "So special. So very special."

He kissed her softly, then raised his head to watch the slow movement of his hands on her neck. Ever downward they crept, trembling slightly, fingers inching under the open tabs of her shirt, gliding downward still. The swell of her breasts inflamed him, but he continued his progress until he reached the knot at her ribs and released it. He spread the soft fabric to the side, easing it wider and wider until her bare breasts were open to his gaze. Holding his breath, he touched her, first the creamy outer contours and soft undersides, then the nipples, taut and puckered. He brushed the pads of his thumbs over them, watched them tighten more as her breath came faster. A tiny sound came from her throat and he raised his eyes to her look of desire.

"Do you want me?" he whispered, needing to hear the words.

"Oh, yes."

Abandoning her breasts abruptly, he took her hand in his. This time his voice came out in a growl. "I don't think I can tease and play. Come on."

She didn't have to ask where he was leading her. She knew, and she wanted to go. Her pulse raced as she let herself be led through the living room, then down the long hall and into her bedroom. There he caught her in his arms and kissed her fiercely.

Her shirt fell easy prey to his marauding fingers, drifting to the floor, already forgotten. He sank back on the bed and drew her between his knees, his lips closing over one breast with such precision that she cried out in stunned delight. It felt so right, his mouth suckling her while his hands slid hungrily up and down her back. The tip of his tongue darted against her nipple, his teeth gently closed and tugged. A ripple of heat seared through her and settled in her womb, and she clutched his shoulders to hold herself upright. When he took her other nipple between his thumb and forefinger and rolled it around, she muffled a moan against his hair.

Suddenly time was of the essence. Dallas's hands were in her shorts, pushing them and her panties over her hips. He continued to kiss her breasts while he worked blindly at the buttons of his shirt, then his belt, shifting her to lie on the bed for only as long as it took him to shuck his clothes. Then he was back beside her, on her, in her, thrusting powerfully.

Paige welcomed the force. She needed it, if for no other reason than to assure herself she wasn't dreaming. She thrived on it, rose to meet it, found the fireball inside glowing, growing, bursting. Long orgasmic shudders shook her then. She panted, cried raggedly in release. Seconds later Dallas stiffened and moaned, gasping for air as raggedly as she.

He murmured her name brokenly and collapsed over her. "Paige . . . Paige . . . how good it is with you. . . ."

She could do nothing but smile. Where last time she'd been overjoyed simply to reach that exploding pinnacle, this time she took pleasure just as much in Dallas's. To know that he'd wanted her enough to come back, to know that she'd been able to satisfy him again was another feather in her cap. She ran her hands over his damp body and beamed her pride.

"I'm crushing you," he grunted. "God, I don't think I can move."

"Don't. I'm all right."

But he forced himself to his side, turning his head to bask in her satisfaction. The sounds of their labored breathing filled the air, slowing gradually to coincide with the rhythmic pound of the surf beyond the open sliding door. He moved his head on the pillow, then realized that it wasn't linen beneath his ear. "We didn't even pull the spread back. Man, I couldn't think straight." Not then. But now he could. He bolted up on an elbow. "Oh, my God."

Paige raised her head, eyes filled with concern. "What is it?"

"Oh, my God. Paige, I couldn't think straight. It was so fast. I didn't use anything. . . ."

She grasped his shoulder then, gently kneading the tense muscle. "It's all right, Dallas," she said softly. "It'll be okay."

He eyed her strangely. "Don't tell me you rushed out to a doctor this morning."

"I won't. I didn't." She hadn't anticipated the need.

"Then how could it be okay? If I've gotten you pregnant—"

"We'll worry about it then. I told you the other night. The timing's okay for me."

He scowled. "You really think the rhythm method works? Talk about naiveté!" Thrusting a hand through his hair, he sagged back to the bed. "Dumb is dumb. I take the cake when I'm with you. Damn it, if I hadn't wanted you so badly. . ."

"Dallas—"

"It's *Jesse*, damn it! I'm not your chauffeur anymore!"

Gathering her composure, Paige sat up quietly on the bed. "What are you?"

He glowered. "Your lover! Or hadn't you noticed?"

She eyed him steadily. "What are you?"

He stared at her angrily, then bounded up and reached for his jeans. "What in the hell are you talking about?"

"I'm talking about you, Jesse. I want to know who you are, what you do, why you're here."

With an impatient tug he zipped his jeans. "You want to know? You really want to know?"

"Yes."

He gritted his teeth. "Well, I'm sure as hell not a chauffeur!"

"I think I knew that," she stated calmly. "Now tell me something I don't know."

"I was at the party the other night."

For the first time her composure wavered. She wasn't sure what she'd expected to hear him say, but it wasn't this. "My show?"

"Yes. Your show. I was there with all the others, dragged along by a friend of mine, a high-priced lawyer who picks up clients at bashes like those."

"I see," she said softly and lowered her head, only to jerk it back up when he exploded.

"No, you don't see! We were standing around, the two of us, drinking the champagne that your host so graciously provided, and we were studying you. My friend had heard rumors." She winced, but he went on. "I told him they were wrong. We made a bet."

Paige swallowed hard. Her insides were trembling in a way totally unrelated to the passion she'd known moments before. "A bet?" she asked, her voice thin.

Dallas had come too far to turn back, not that he was thinking of doing so at the moment. He was angry at the emotions Paige generated. He went on, aiming to hurt. "A bet that I could make it with you. Looks like I won."

He didn't feel like a winner. He felt like a snake. Unable to stand himself for a minute longer in the confines of the room, he whirled on his bare heel and stormed out.

Paige shook all over. Creeping jerkily to the edge of the bed, she strained down for her blouse, then held it to her breasts and slowly rocked back and forth. She stared at the door, then the floor. She took several deep, shuddering breaths.

Out on the deck, Dallas was in no better shape. He hated himself, hated her for causing it. No, he corrected, he didn't hate her. It was what he felt that he hated. Tender. Possessive. And aching to soothe the hurt he'd caused.

She hadn't asked for him. Not once had she been the seducer. She was happy with her life. Who was he to mess it up? Oh, sure, he'd taught her something about herself. She knew now that she was capable of true passion. So what in the devil was she supposed to do with it?

Bending over, he propped his hands on the wood railing. The sea looked stormy, or was it simply a reflection of the turbulence within himself? He didn't know what to do, whether to leave or stay, whether to apologize or forget he'd ever said a word. The most compassionate thing he could do now was to get out of her life. She'd forget him. She'd find someone who was warm enough, caring enough, man enough to give her the love she deserved. He couldn't. Love wasn't part of his vocabulary. He didn't want the responsibility of a wife, much less children. If she was pregnant, he didn't know what he'd do!

For a long time he stood there brooding. The air cooled with the lowering of the sun, but he welcomed the chill on his bare chest as a reminder of the cold-hearted soul that he was. They'd all been right. He was a bastard. In *every* sense of the word.

He jumped when he felt a hand on his shoulder and whirled to find Paige with his shirt. She'd dressed, this time wearing a crewneck sweater and high socks with her shorts. Her face was pale. He could see remnants of moisture on her lower lids.

"You'll catch cold," she murmured, reaching to drape the shirt across his shoulders. Taking the shirt from her, he put it on, buying time as he carefully secured the four lower buttons.

"After what I've done, I'd have thought you'd be pleased if I caught pneumonia."

"I wouldn't."

"You should. I'm a lout. You deserve someone better."

"I'm not looking for someone. And you couldn't catch pneumonia. It's too warm and you're too strong."

Her beneficence ate at him. He took her shoulders, tempted to try to shake some sense into her. She should scream at him, kick him out. But she didn't. And he couldn't shake her, not when he felt suddenly so very tired. "Paige," he said, sighing quietly, "didn't any of what I said bother you?"

"Of course it bothered me. I'm human. No one likes to feel cheap."

He winced. "God, don't use that word." His fingers bit into her shoulders. "It wasn't like that. I swear. It may have started with a bet, but I'd never have made the bet in the first place if you hadn't appealed to me from the start. Bet or no, I'd probably have sought you out. It was the air of challenge surrounding the bet that made me pose as your chauffeur. I'm usually more direct."

"I'm sure."

"Damn it, how can you be so calm! Yell at me, Paige! Tell me what a jackass I am!"

"That's not my way. Of course, if you insist on a tantrum, I could probably muster a feeble one. Should I try?" The corners of her lips were twitching. She was trying her best not to smile. Yes, Dallas had hurt her, but she didn't have it in her heart to carry on. It was as though she sensed that an inner demon was eating him, that he didn't want to be this way, that he didn't *have* to be this way. And, in spite of everything, he did make her feel like a woman. She couldn't find fault with that.

He scowled at her, closed his eyes and shook his head, then gently enfolded her in his arms and held her against him. He felt her catch her breath and resist for an instant, but only an instant. Slowly she relaxed. The faint shudder that passed through her suggested that she was more sensitive than she let on. Once again he told himself to leave, but his arms wouldn't listen. They simply held her tighter, rocking her gently.

"Paige, Paige, Paige. What am I going to do with you? You're a fool to put up with someone like me."

"I'm not 'putting up' with you. You're just . . . here."

"Same difference. I don't want to hurt you, really I don't, it's just that I don't have much experience with gentleness."

She drew her head back and looked up at him. "What do you do, Jesse, when you're not masquerading as a chauffeur?"

He smiled. It was nice, holding her like this, passion spent, simply...close. He couldn't remember ever having done anything like it. "I'm a film editor."

"Feature films?"

"Documentaries, mostly."

"Are you between jobs?"

"You could say that. I'm on vacation. When I work, it's pretty intensive. I finished something a week ago and I need a break."

"What was it that you finished?"

"A documentary on prison reform. Pretty depressing considering the footage I had to leave on the floor in order to keep the tone the producer wanted."

"Not much reform, huh?"

His features tightened. He focused unseeing on the ribbing of her sweater. "Not much. I mean, they're working at it, but it's like trying to plug a three-foot leak with a toothpick. Conditions inside this country's prisons are terrifying and getting worse."

"They're better than in many other countries."

"That doesn't excuse it. This is America. We pride ourselves on being progressive. Let me tell you, the stuff on that film was discouraging."

"Do you feel that the finished product is deceptive?"

"No. Not deceptive. It told the truth. Maybe not the whole truth—" he met her gaze "—but then, many of us are guilty of that from time to time." He took a measured breath. "I never lied to you at any point, Paige. I mean, when you asked me about driving and all, I never lied."

"I know," she said softly. "Don't worry about it. You've told me the whole truth now, haven't you?"

It was his chance. Holding her slightly away, he rubbed her upper arms for a minute. Then he dropped them and pressed his palms to the wood rail behind him. There was a fierceness underlying the quiet in his tone. "I'm a loner, Paige. I don't want you or any other woman tying up my life. I can't be expected to give. I don't have it in me. For as many times as we're together, one day I'll pick up and be gone. I can promise you nothing."

In an uncharacteristic burst of anger, she tipped up her chin. "I thought I told you that I didn't want anything. Weren't you listening? Or did you simply chalk off my words to female nonsense? Well, I was serious, Dallas. I'm not asking a *thing* of you. I didn't ask you to drive me around New York, or to kiss me outside my front door." She held up a hand to ward off a retort. "I know, I know. I kissed you back, but I only took what was offered. I didn't ask for a thing. I never have. I never will. I have my pride, too. And my house, my life, my career. I'm perfectly capable of taking care of myself with or without you!"

Throwing her hands in the air, she half turned, muttering, "Of all the egotistical—" Then she caught herself and whirled back, hair flying. "And if you're so worried about demands I might make, why don't you climb back into that grotesque limousine—" she pointed toward the front of the house with a shaking hand "—and race back to New York." She shook her head and began muttering again. "God, I've never seen anything like it. Must be urban insanity. Why is it that city people think life revolves around them? There is more to life than *you*, Jesse Dallas." She stared at him for another minute, then, wearing a look of exasperation, stalked to the far side of the deck and faced the darkening sea.

Jesse came up quietly beside her. "I wasn't sure you could do that."

"Do what?"

"Let loose."

"Now you know."

"Mmm, so I do."

"I don't do it often," she cautioned, calming almost miraculously. She'd blown up and was done. That was all there was to it. "You've been treated to a rare show."

"Then I'll treasure it all the more."

Feeling very much herself again, she slanted him a look. "Are you hungry?"

"Where did *that* come from?"

"I haven't eaten since ten."

"See what happens when you don't have a chauffeur to look after you."

"I always do it this way. Brunch at ten, dinner at six. Two meals. Very healthy."

He arched a brow. "I wonder. You must be starved."

"I've got some fresh sole in the refrigerator. I thought I'd broil it in lemon butter. Sound okay?"

"You're inviting me to dinner?"

"Unless you have other plans. You did mention you had friends in the area."

"They're in Gloucester and they don't know I'm here."

"You were going to surprise them, too?"

Her smug tone goaded him. "I hadn't even thought of them," he growled. "I came to see you. You know that."

"If that's the case, why not join me for dinner?"

"I'd rather take you out."

"Afraid of my cooking? I'm pretty good."

"I'm sure you are. But I didn't come here to put you to work."

They were back to square one. "Why *did* you come, Jesse?" she asked, teasing forgotten. Even the dimming light couldn't hide the urgency on her face.

He took a deep breath, then let it slowly out and raised his eyes to the sky. "I'm not quite sure." His gaze leveled. "I needed to see you, to be with you. I needed a vacation from—" he gestured vaguely south-ward "—from all that. It was an impulse, I suppose. Hell, I'm not sure why I came!"

"Do you want to spend the night?"

"Of course I want to spend the night!"

"Are you good with your hands?"

He stared at her in disbelief for a minute, then abruptly shifted gears. "You *know* I'm good with my hands."

Unfazed by his innuendo, she plugged on. "Can you fix things?"

The drawl receded. "That depends on what they are."

"Wood planks. Several of the lower ones near the beach are loose. Several others need to be replaced. There's also a faucet that drips in the kitchen, and the bathroom door sticks."

"You need a handyman."

"If I had one, I wouldn't be asking you, would I?"

"No."

"Well? Can you make yourself useful while I work tomorrow?"

"You're gonna work? I was hoping we could drive along the coast, maybe stop at a little place for lobster—"

"I'm gonna work. You're the one who's on vacation, not me."

"All work and no play—"

"Do you want the sole? It won't be fresh much longer, and—"

"You're starved. I know. All right. Broil your damned sole." He watched her start across the deck. "But I'll get that lobster with you one day." He spoke louder as she disappeared through the doorway. "You can't carve stone all the time . . . !"

THEY ATE at the lacquered table in the dining room, seated comfortably in contemporary armchairs opposite each other. It wasn't a heavily romantic dinner; there were no candles, no fresh flowers. But it was pleasant, companionable. When Jesse wanted to know more about Marblehead, Paige indulged him. In turn, when she wanted to hear more about his work, he opened up.

"It's a lonely job, high on pressure. But it's fascinating. Challenging."

"How did you get into it?"

"Actually, I was a photographer. Straight out of high school. I'd been free-lancing to support the habit, but I didn't have enough money for college, so I decided to work for a couple of years. I guess I did okay. Enough of my pictures were picked up by the Associated Press for them to eventually take me on staff. From there things seemed to never stop." He snorted. "I wanted to see the world. I sure did. All the hot spots—Iran, Rhodesia, Vietnam, the Philippines. I was young and energetic. Anywhere the other photographers didn't want to go, I went."

"It must have been enlightening."

"To say the least. Oh, there were pleasant stops on the tour. I saw most of Europe and places in this country that I'd never seen. But for the most part I was sent to trouble spots. Enlightening? That's one word for it. Poverty, squalor, repression, revolution—it's frightening what goes on in the world."

"I'd think you'd burn out after a while."

"I did, though at the time I refused to admit it. I told myself that it was simply time to go back to school."

"College?"

"Mmm. I had enough money saved and, though I'd always been an avid reader, something inside me insisted on a formal education."

"What was it . . . that something?"

He thought for a while before answering. "Pride, I suppose. I came from nothing, but I wanted to be as

good if not better than the next guy, and a college education seemed one step toward that."

"How old were you?"

"Twenty-seven and a hell of a lot older than most of
my classmates, I can tell you. If I hadn't been so determined, I think I'd have dropped out after the first se-
mester. It was hard going back to it cold."

"But you made it."

"Uh-huh. And I discovered film editing in the process." His thoughts tripped back and he smiled. "I had
this fantastic professor. Very bright guy. Real dry wit.
We hit it off from the start. He got me my first job."

"He must be proud that you've continued in the
field."

The smile faded. "He's dead. Had a heart attack one
day and—" he snapped his fingers "—he was gone."

"I'm sorry."

Jesse shrugged. "That's the way it is. Anyway, he's
left his legacy. And my career has soared."

Listening to him talk, studying the changing expres-
sions on his face, Paige saw that Jesse was an expert at
denying pain. She guessed that he'd been very fond of
this professor, but that to say that he missed him would
have been to acknowledge the sorrow of his death. Jesse
was hard; the things he'd seen in his days as a photographer must have trained him all too well, she mused.

"What are some of the other films you've edited?" she
asked, hoping to spark his enthusiasm again. Her ploy
didn't quite work.

He frowned wryly. "Let's see. There was a documentary on child abuse, one on kiddie porn. I did a super thing on suicide. And the elderly—chronicling their

plight in a society that thrives on youthfulness was interesting. Then there was a thing on political corruption that turned a lot of heads."

"If it was anything like *Follow the Leader*, I can imagine."

"You saw *Follow the Leader*?"

"Uh-huh. Last winter."

"What did you think?"

"It was riveting. Fascinating like a good horror flick, all the more terrifying because it wasn't. I thought it was well-done. Totally effective."

"Thank you."

Her eyes widened. "It was yours?" She smiled in delight at discovering now just how talented he was. "Oh, dear, what if I'd said it was terrible?"

"If that had been your honest opinion, I'd have accepted it."

"You accept a lot, don't you?"

"What choice have I got?"

She knew that he was right in a way. One couldn't fight things one couldn't change. But she was sorry to see the matter-of-factness his words implied. There was such a thing as feeling—feeling happy or sad, relieved or disappointed. Dallas felt; she knew he did. The faint smile that had touched his lips when he'd thanked her for praising *Follow the Leader* told her that he'd been pleased.

Concentrating on other feelings she was sure existed, she jumped back to the enumeration he'd given her of his work. She'd heard the sarcasm in his voice. "Do you have a choice as to what films you work on?"

"I can always say no."

"You sounded cynical before. Does it depress you when you work on films like those?"

"What depresses me is that the conditions exposed in those films exist. The work itself is great. I like what I do."

"You mentioned pressure. Where does it come in?"

"The producer may want one thing, the director may get another. I've got to work my tail off to try to please them both *and* produce something that doesn't look like it's been edited. It's worse with feature films, technically speaking. Between special effects and places where the viewer has to be tricked into believing something happened that really didn't—"

"Like what?" Enrapt, Paige propped her elbow on the table, her chin in her palm.

For the first time in the discussion, Jesse's eyes twinkled. "Like when the heroine is supposed to be swinging across an open gorge on a vine. She doesn't really, y'know. She'll be shown pulling back to leap with vine in hand, holding her breath, looking terrified. Then the frame will switch to a companion or a pursuer. By the time the audience sees the heroine again, she's falling in a heap, safe but shaky, on the other side of the gorge."

"That's sneaky."

"That's often the way it works."

"How can you bear to go to the movies, knowing all that's probably gone on in the cutting room? Isn't it disillusioning?"

He grinned. "Not necessarily. I do what the rest of the audience does. I choose to believe. That's what entertainment's all about. Take singing. You've got this beautiful gal belting out a soulful ballad. She's oozing love or anger or heartbreak. You know damn well it's just a song, but you believe she's in agony. You also know that she's practiced singing the song this way a thousand times and that she'll sing it this way a thousand more times. And that if one song's sad, the next one will probably be happy."

"Isn't it possible she's singing from the heart?"

"Not likely. And she sure as hell's not singing to you like it seems."

"I think you wish she were," Paige said, a daring smile on her face.

"Me? Are you kidding? Not me!"

"I'm not so sure," she mused, standing to gather the dishes. As she headed for the kitchen she added a teasing note to her voice. "I think you might like to have a woman so in love with you that she'd pour out her heart and soul that way."

She heard a low grumble, that was all. Smiling to herself, she decided that it might be good for him to have a woman like that. He struck her as a man who'd been alone too long, who'd seen too much of the dark side of life. He'd been right when he'd said that he needed a break from all that. Perhaps a few days here at her beach house might brighten his outlook.

When she returned with a tray bearing coffee and healthy slabs of blueberry pie, she cocked her head toward the deck. Jesse quickly took the tray and she led the way. Moments later they were seated at the small table there, sheltered from the sea breeze by the wide overhang. A porch light behind them cast a warm glow.

The full moon did the rest. In the background the surf serenaded.

Jesse sat back in his chair and inhaled deeply. "It's lovely here."

"Relaxing?"

"Mmm."

"Vacationlike?"

Rather than agreeing a second time, he found himself staring at her. "You like living alone. Won't my being here cramp your style?"

"It'll be a novelty. Besides, you won't be here very long."

His gaze narrowed. "How do you know?"

"You've already told me you'll pick up one day and be gone."

"But if that day comes later rather than sooner?"

"Then . . . it'll be an experience. If worse comes to worst and you get on my nerves, I'll send you packing."

He leaned forward and spoke in a very low, very sober voice. "Do you realize what you're doing, Paige? You're inviting me to spend my vacation here."

"I'm not inviting. You showed up and you seem to like the place. I'm simply saying that you can stay if you'd like. I'm not so selfish that I can't share for a little while. It's a big place."

"You're generous."

"What're friends for?"

"We're lovers, Paige. You haven't forgotten that, have you?"

She spoke more softly. "No."

"And if I stay here I won't be sleeping in the guest room."

"I didn't expect that you would."

He sat back then, his expression grim. "Why are you doing this?"

"Offering my house—"

"And yourself—"

"Because I like you. Does there have to be another reason?"

"There usually is."

"Oh, look," she said, sighing, "I'd get all huffy again but one show of high spirits a day is all I can manage. The fact is that you're welcome to stay here if you want. If you don't, you can leave. The decision's yours. It's no big thing."

For what seemed an eternity to Paige, he pondered her words. When she could stand no more of his silence, she taunted, "What's the matter, Jesse? Are you afraid of my feelings, or your own?"

"I'm not afraid."

"Then why the dilemma? There aren't any strings attached to my offer. Take it or leave it."

"You're a cool cookie."

"So are you."

"Which means that we might actually survive in each other's presence for more than a day? I've never lived with anyone before."

"You're not *living* with me. You're just . . . staying in my house."

"And you're playing with words."

She sighed again, this time with fatigue. "Maybe so. But not anymore. I intend to eat my pie, drink my coffee, clean up the mess in the kitchen, then sit down with a book. Okay?"

Jesse couldn't help but smile at the question she'd tacked on at the end, as if she were asking his permission when he knew very well that she'd do what she wanted. It was, indeed, her house, her life.

Yes, she could eat her pie, drink her coffee, clean up the mess in the kitchen, then sit down with a book. And, yes, he would stay for a time, if for no other reason than to prove to them both that he could handle it, then leave, as he'd promised.

5

JESSE WAS THE ONE who sat with a book, but it was the following afternoon, and he wasn't reading. He was staring out over the deck, thinking of the night before. For all the indifference she showed at times, Paige had been as impassioned as ever in bed. It was as though the softest side of her came out then, softest and wildest. For a woman who'd never known the fullness of love-making, she was a marvel. Making up for lost time, perhaps. Perhaps simply high on new discoveries. Whatever, he was pleased. And so he sat there with no desire to leave.

Oh, yes, he'd begun work on the chores she'd suggested. Early that morning—well, it had seemed early to him, since it was soon after he'd awoken, though Paige had been in her studio for hours—they'd gone into town to pick up the tools and materials he'd needed. He grinned, remembering the pseudoargument they'd had before they'd left.

"I'll drive," she'd proclaimed, slipping her car keys from their hook.

"You will not. I won't have a woman toting me around. *I'll* drive."

"I'm sorry. That limousine may have been fine for the city, but I won't be seen in it around here. Besides, there'd be nowhere to park. It's too big."

"*I'll drive,*" he'd insisted, taking her arm and all but dragging her out of the house.

"My car, then," she'd grumbled, pressing her keys into his hand. He'd promptly pocketed them in exchange for his own. On the front walk moments later she'd dug in her heels. And stared. Then slanted him a dry gaze. "No limousine. Cute."

"The limousine went back the other night. I do have wheels of my own."

"So I see. Not bad, for an MG. A little old, perhaps, but not bad."

"Not old. Vintage."

She'd shrugged. "If you say so."

"Would you bad-mouth Victoria?"

"Oh, Lord, it's got a name."

"Of course it does. And I won't have it taken in vain."

"You should have told me you drove your own car up here."

"But then we wouldn't be standing here arguing. I love it when you get worked up. Your freckles stand out."

She'd stared at him, then finally thrown up her hands in a gesture of helplessness. "You're impossible."

"Mmm. That's what I've been trying to tell you. Come on. I thought you had work to do. If we don't get these errands done— Listen, I really can go myself."

"You don't know the way. I'll show you this time, then next time you'll be on your own."

"What did I ever do without you?" he'd muttered, tongue-in-cheek, as he'd pressed her into the MG.

They'd stopped at the hardware store, the lumberyard, the supermarket and the dock. Fortunately she'd only given him momentary argument when he insisted on paying for everything they bought. He wouldn't be a kept man—he felt strongly about that. She must have sensed it.

At Paige's insistence, they'd made one other stop. Jesse had argued that he'd be more than willing to take the responsibility for birth control, but she'd been firm. She didn't trust him, she'd teased, eyes twinkling. So, leaving him to wait—by choice—in the car, she ran in to see her doctor.

At least she'd be protected, he mused now. He didn't care how it happened, but he wanted her safe. Unwanted pregnancies were high on his list of prohibitions. There were far too many children born into the world to parents who either lacked the desire or capacity to give them what they needed. He knew all about that. He knew about it all too well.

Frustrated with the turn of his thoughts, he stood up on the deck and stretched, then on impulse headed for Paige's studio. He'd only seen it once, that first night when she'd given him a quick tour of the house. He wanted to see it again now.

The door was open. He came to a halt on its threshold, as though barred by an invisible gate. This room, like the others on the ocean side of the house, was fully skylit. The outer walls were glass. On a summer day such as this the sliding doors were open, allowing large screens to admit the breeze. Though there was central air-conditioning in the house, Jesse suspected that Paige rarely used it. She didn't have to. The ocean air was more than adequate.

It wasn't the airiness of the room that held him still. It was the emotional atmosphere. There was a serenity here, a sense of peace. His eye roamed, touching on tools and raw materials, workbenches, pedestals, a wide desk. An occasional poster, well framed, hung on white plastered walls. A large bulletin board bearing miscellaneous drawings and notes held on with push-pins hung over the desk.

Inevitably, though, his gaze came to rest on Paige. She sat on a stool at the far end of the room. A large piece of burlap fully covered her lap. Atop it lay a piece of wood, cushioned securely in the notch between her thighs. She wore a face shield, a piece of clear plastic that hung from a headpiece and extended beyond her chin. In one hand she held a mallet, in the other a gouge. Putting mallet to gouge to wood, she hammered gently, rhythmically. After several moments she stopped, lifted the piece to study what she'd done, replaced it on her lap, turning it slightly, and began to hammer again.

So engrossed was she in her work, so obviously content, that he couldn't disturb her. He turned and was about to leave when she caught sight of him and slid her mask back to the top of her head.

"Don't go."

"I didn't mean to bother you."

"You're no bother. I need a break, anyway."

"What are you working on?" He didn't budge from the door. It seemed he'd be trespassing otherwise.

She glanced down at the wood in her lap and ran her hand over it. "It's the first of a group of sandpipers."

"A group. Mmm, you did have several groups of other kinds of things in your show, didn't you?"

"So you did see something besides me that night," she teased. He simply arched his brows and tipped his head sideways in confirmation. She hesitated for just a minute. "What did you think?"

"Your work is beautiful. Filled with feeling. That was one of the reasons I was so convinced you weren't . . . well, you know."

"Yes," she admitted quietly. "Jesse?"

"Hmm?"

Her eyes twinkled. "You can come in."

"In? Oh. Sure." The invisible gate opened. He took several steps forward. He still felt like an intruder encroaching on a very private, serene world, but she'd made the offer, and the peace of it was too good to pass up. Planting his hands in the pockets of his jeans, he rocked back on his bare heels and made a quick sweep of the room. "This is a nice place to work. Very bright . . . pleasant."

She followed the path of his gaze. "Actually, it's the master bedroom. Or was. But from the first time I saw the house, this room struck me as an ideal studio. It's large and has plenty of work space. The walk-in closet is terrific for storage. And the bathroom supplies all the running water I need." She glanced toward the alcove in question. "I had the door taken off so it becomes part of the room." The bathroom itself was huge and multifaceted. What was now open held two sinks and abundant counter space. The bath, shower and commode were behind separate doors.

Jesse began to move quietly around the room, studying more closely those things he'd glimpsed from the door. He paused at the workbench, above which were mounted a mind-boggling assortment of tools. "You use all these?"

"At one point or another."

"They look alike." Reaching out, he ran his hand across a neat lineup of metal somethings.

"Those are rasps. Each one is just a little different from the next. When it comes to the fine work on a piece, the small differences are critical."

He moved on to a cluster of what looked to be cloth strips.

"Abrasives," she explained before he could ask. "They can be kept wide or cut thinner. I use them for smoothing and finishing when I'm working in wood."

"I'd have thought you'd use sandpaper."

"Perhaps once in a while. But those strips are more sensitive, more gentle."

Nodding, he left the bench and approached her. His gaze was on her lap. "What kind of wood is that?"

She lifted the roughly carved chunk and turned it slowly. "Walnut."

"Will the other sandpipers be walnut, too?"

"Uh-huh. Each one will be slightly different, though. No two pieces of wood—or stone—are identical. For that matter, no single piece is entirely predictable."

Considering her words, he looked back toward the desk. "You make sketches beforehand?"

"Uh-huh. Go look. The sandpipers are right on top."

Crossing to the desk, he studied the drawings. On a large single sheet were solo birds, then clusters. Far from detailed, they merely outlined the general shapes she sought. "Very pretty. Light."

"That's what I'm hoping for. Sandpipers always look like little imps scurrying along the sand. I'd like to catch some of that movement."

"In a stationary form?"

"Sure. It's all in the shape of the bird, its attitude, the placement of its feet."

He nodded, intrigued. "What will you mount them on?"

"Sand, I hope. Glue does wonders for immobilizing tiny grains."

"Should be very effective." He walked back to her. "Most of the things on exhibit the other night were larger. Are you changing your style?"

"Just varying it. I'd like the sandpipers to be life-size."

"But not in exact detail." None of her things were fully realistic; he'd learned that at the show. It was the interpretation she brought to seemingly common objects that made her work unique.

"No. It's the general form I want, a fluidity to enhance that sense of movement. The eye follows lines, curves, changes in tone and color. It's the rhythm of this eye movement that brings the piece to life." She paused, thinking aloud. "I may blend two birds together. I'm not sure. It depends on how the wood responds."

"So you play it by ear?"

"Uh-huh. Spontaneity can be exciting."

"Then you don't always know what you're going to do when you get started?"

"I have vague ideas. But I have to be flexible. Every piece of wood, every slab of stone has flaws. If I suddenly find a weak spot, I've got to work around it. Compensate, so to speak."

Stepping back to lean against the workbench, Jesse crossed his arms over his chest. "Do you ever run into a problem and have to chuck the whole thing?"

"Once in a while. Fortunately the worst flaws usually show up in the early stages. It'd be heartbreaking to do all the work only to find, at the end, that the piece was hopelessly weak."

"I can imagine." He found himself studying the mask atop her head. It pulled her hair back from her face so that even at work she looked pretty. "Do you always wear that plastic shield when you work?"

"At this stage in the piece, yes. It'd be too easy for chips of wood to come flying up at me. By the time I get past roughing out and shaping, it's not necessary. The finishing work is safer. At least with wood. When it comes to stone and I'm using hand drills for refinement, there's a whole lot of dust. If it's really bad I wear a respirator." She glanced around her. "That's one of the reasons this room is so perfect. The ventilation's great."

Jesse took it all in, his gaze returning time and again to Paige. She looked so . . . content sitting there cradling her work. She seemed perfectly willing to answer his questions, and there were more he wanted to ask. But she had to work. Much as he'd like it if she quit for the day and spent time with him, he couldn't ask. He knew how he resented interruptions when he worked, and he didn't want to risk being the object of *her* eventual resentment.

Good intentions intact, he straightened and was walking toward the door when a small stone piece caught his eye. It lay on one of the auxiliary worktables to one side of the room. He stopped, picked it up, stared at it.

"What's this?"

"It's...it's just something I was fooling around with," she offered a bit too quickly.

He sent her a curious glance, then looked back at the stone. It was slightly larger than his hand, longer than it was wide or tall. One part of the top had been carved; it was this portion that held his attention. He scrutinized it cautiously, looked down at his own hand, then again at the stone. He saw them clearly—two fingers, with a third on the way. They were masculine.

Wondering when she'd started the piece but half-afraid to ask, he set down the stone and walked thoughtfully from the studio. Barefoot, he moved silently through the house, across the deck and down the wood stairs to the beach. The tide was high. He skirted its lacy edge, picking his way over stones and seaweed, through random rock clusters. When he reached a large boulder, he rested against it.

That was where Paige found him moments later.

"I thought you might be here," she said, approaching with considerable hesitance. "Can I...can I join you?"

The gaze that searched her features conveyed far greater intensity than the shrug he gave. "It's your beach."

"I won't disturb you if you'd rather be alone." When he shrugged a second time, she averted her eyes. "I wanted to explain," she said quietly, looking toward the horizon. "That was . . . your hand."

"I wondered."

"I started it yesterday."

"Why?"

It was her turn to shrug. She looked down at the pebbles underfoot. "I don't know. I was walking out here and saw the stone. The vision just came."

"Is that how it happens?"

"Not always. Sometimes I have an idea and spend months searching for the right piece to carve it from." Her eyes lit up. "Other times the piece itself generates the idea. It's like..." Self-consciously she let her words trail off.

"Like what?"

When she still hesitated, Jesse smiled softly and gave her a coaxing nod. She resumed in a shy murmur, "It's like the stone speaks to me. Her cheeks grew pink. She knew she probably sounded overly esoteric, but she desperately wanted to share her feelings with Jesse. "Like it's got a...a secret just waiting, waiting in there." She lowered her voice to a near-whisper. "The secret's often very special, very private. There are times when I hesitate to carve it out, almost feeling as if I'm betraying something the stone might not want revealed."

"Then why do you do it?" he asked gently.

"I don't know. Compulsion maybe. Maybe for the satisfaction of proving that what I saw was there. Maybe just because it is there and it's too beautiful to keep hidden."

"My hand's here in real life. Why replicate it in stone?"

"Because it *is* beautiful. And . . . because there's something to be said for the continuity of nature."

He reached out then and, curling his fingers around her neck, brought her closer. He slipped his arm around her shoulders, pulling her down to sit by his side against the boulder.

"Does that mean you'd carve other parts of my body?"

"It'd be a challenge."

His breath teased her brow. "For me, too. I'm not sure I could take it—your hands on me like that."

"My hands would be on the stone."

"Yeah, and the stone would be like a voodoo doll. I'd feel everything."

She grinned. "What if I just stuck with something innocent, like your shoulders."

"You'd sculpt a pair of shoulders? Boo-hiss."

"Then . . . a torso." She touched his chest, drew her hand down to his waist. "It's very fit."

"You're getting hotter. So am I."

She saw the direction of his thoughts, "Jesse Dallas, I wouldn't sculpt that!"

"Why not? Michelangelo did it any number of times."

"You were the one who spoke of voodoo dolls. How would you feel if I did what you're suggesting?"

"Just like stone. Damned . . . hard."

Chuckling, she turned to him and buried her face against his shirt. He'd begun to gently caress her back. It felt good. "That's one of the reasons I wouldn't do it."

"And the other?"

She tipped her head back and met his gaze. "Some secrets really are too private. Some I just don't want to share."

He growled deeply, as though he was in pain, and swung her from her seat and around until she stood between his spread knees, her slender body arched, her arms circling his back.

Her lips were soft and moist. Unable to resist their silent invitation, he lowered his own in a kiss filled with magic. At least Paige thought it was magic, because suddenly and fully every one of her senses came alive.

Similarly affected, Jesse dug his fingers into her bottom and pressed her intimately to his hips. "What do you think of *that*?" he drawled.

"Just like stone. Damned . . . hard."

He laughed, a deep rumbling laugh. She didn't hear him laugh often, certainly not like that. It was a good sound, a healthy sound filled with pleasure and appreciation. It made her feel very glad that he was here.

When he lowered his mouth to murmur in her ear, his voice came out more gravelly than ever. "How about if we go in and try out that toy the doctor gave you this morning?"

"I'm working," she teased, knowing full well she'd do no more sculpting today, knowing full well she didn't want to.

"I'll give you plenty to work on. You can touch everything. Y'know, memorize shapes and textures and—"

"I get the idea. But we'd better hurry or you'll have to carry me all the way up to the house. My legs don't do well under this kind of strain." The strain she spoke of was heady. Her breasts were already swelling against the firmness of his chest. Her ribs felt every breath he took. She couldn't help but respond to the slow undulation of his hips. Her insides were molten.

Before she could do more than catch her breath, Jesse swung her up into his arms.

"Hey!" She squirmed. "I'm not incapacitated yet!"

He grinned. "It's my machismo seeping out. Indulge me."

She indulged him everything, but the indulgence was far from one-sided, for he was as giving a lover as ever.

Much later, after they'd showered and dressed and dined on sautéed scallops, fresh broccoli and potatoes, they sat down in the living room to read. Paige couldn't remember spending a more relaxed evening. She was doing nothing that she wouldn't normally do, yet it was different. She felt warm and content, and wondered if it had anything to do with the man sitting at his own end of the sofa engrossed in a book he'd chosen from her shelf. How incredibly comfortable it had been having Jesse around.

She enjoyed telling him about her work, voicing feelings she'd previously held private. She enjoyed the banter that sparked easily between them, even that of a sexual nature, so new to her yet such fun. She enjoyed the way he held her, the way he touched her with exquisite tenderness one time, with fiery need another. Whether protectively gentle or wild with demand, he made her feel that she was the only woman in the world.

Of course, it wasn't true. He'd had women before and he'd have them again. She knew that; she accepted it.

But when he gave of himself, he gave fully. And he was giving to her now. So what if he'd leave one day? She'd simply return to the life she'd had before and be all the fuller for what she and Jesse had shared. She was lucky, very lucky. Life continued to treat her well.

THE NEXT TWO WEEKS were unbelievably wonderful. Having lived so long alone, Paige was astonished at how easily she adapted to having Jesse around. He took care of everything around the house, freeing her to work so that they'd have more time to spend together, which they did.

They ate out often, at Jesse's insistence and expense, and he continued to pay for all of the groceries that entered the house. Page teased that he was buying her off so she'd let him watch the basketball play-offs on television, but she knew that his pride would allow him no other course.

They drove south to Boston, north to the quaint coastal towns of Maine. They took in a movie one evening, rented a boat and went sailing another. They even attended a party given by one of Paige's friends, where Jesse blended in beautifully and enjoyed himself, to boot. Paige felt particularly happy that night, happy and proud and complete.

But the times she most treasured were when she and Jesse were alone at home, sitting together in the living room or on the deck, often at sunset when the sky was indigo and the sea reflected burnished golds from the west.

Those were the times when they talked, when she was able to indulge her curiosity about the man who'd fit into her life with such ease. She wanted to hear more about his work, and she listened, fascinated, as he related anecdotes and adventures.

He had a streak of cynicism. She'd learned that early on, and it emerged regularly during these storytelling sessions. But increasingly, as the days passed, she was aware that he said nothing about his family or childhood. And she began to wonder. It was only natural that, one evening on the deck, she asked him directly.

"Tell me about your family, Jesse."

He looked at her sharply, then curbed what appeared to be censure. But he didn't speak, simply stared across the deck.

"You never mention them," she coaxed in her most gentle tone. "I want to know what it was like for you growing up."

"Why?"

"I'm curious." When he shot her a quelling stare, she refused to be cowed. "Blame it on the artist in me. I'm forever looking beneath the surface of things. God only knows I've talked about myself enough. I mean, you've heard all the little stories about my childhood, you've seen the way I live day-to-day, you've met my friends. It's only fair that you give me a glimpse of you."

"I thought I was doing that," he said coolly, and for the first time Paige felt a twinge of apprehension. He'd been dispassionate before, back when he'd felt called upon to convince her that he had nothing to offer but one day at a time. Then it hadn't bothered her. Now it did. She cared for him, cared deeply. And the more resistant he was to talking about himself, the more badly she wanted to know.

"You let me see Jesse the adult," she reasoned softly. "You tell me about your work. But it's as though from high school back there's nothing. Well, there has to be something. A person doesn't suddenly become eighteen without living through the years before." When she saw that he remained silent, she stood up and waved him away. "Okay, don't tell me. It must be some secret you're keeping. Either that or you're ashamed—" She'd started to walk toward the house when he caught her wrist and held it firmly.

"It's no secret. And I'm not ashamed. It's just . . . difficult to talk about, y'know?"

The chill in his voice had eased. Paige let herself be drawn down onto the lounge beside him. It was a tight fit, but she welcomed the closeness. It was as though he needed it at that particular moment, and his need was a statement in itself.

"I didn't have quite the life you had."

"That's okay. I told you, I was lucky. Where did you grow up?"

"On the wrong side of the tracks."

"Where were the tracks?"

"Delaware. Outside Wilmington. My mother was a hooker. My father wasn't there to watch. There was just my older brother—half brother, actually—and me. He left as soon as he could and then I was alone."

Paige struggled to contain her dismay. "Your mother must have been there sometimes."

"Why 'must'?" he asked, cynicism narrowing to pure bitterness. "As far as she was concerned, bringing me into the world was enough. I never heard the end of it. She told me how she'd hated being pregnant, how her labor had been long and hard. Nine months she'd given me. In her book that was the supreme sacrifice."

"But when you were an infant *someone* had to take care of you."

"Someone did. I don't know who, but someone did. By the time I was old enough to remember, I was being passed from one sitter to the next. My mother showed up from time to time to grudgingly pay the bill, but she was more than happy to leave again. I cramped her style. She told me *that* more than once."

"Didn't your father do something?"

"How innocent you are, Paige. You assume that a parent has to care. Well, he doesn't. And mine didn't . . . *neither* of them. My father was off somewhere doing his own thing. I never knew him."

"Oh, Jesse, I'm sorry. . . ."

"I don't need your pity," he grated. "I survived."

"How? What happened?"

"It was a great relief for my mother when I got old enough to go to school. Fewer sitters to pay. She splurged once a year and bought me clothes. Of course, it didn't matter that there were holes in the knees by Christmas or that by April the pants were inches too short. She felt she was being very generous. Once in a while I got hand-me-downs from neighbors. They still had holes in the knees but at least they fit."

He paused and shifted his arms around her; she suspected he'd momentarily forgotten her presence. "When I was ten I got this one jacket that I loved. She found it on sale. It was a winter jacket and had a furry lining. I used to stick my hands inside the zipper—I told the other kids it was to keep them warm, which made sense since I didn't have mittens, but it was the fur I loved. So soft and warm. I used to sleep with that jacket beside me, turned inside out. It was my teddy bear, my security blanket. I used to imagine being in a world completely surrounded by that fur." He gave a deep, unsteady sigh. Then, with the blink of an eye, he was back in the present.

"I don't know why in the hell I'm telling you this," he growled, but he didn't let her go. "You must think I'm crazy. A ten-year-old hugging an inside-out jacket to fall asleep—"

"Is that what she told you? That it was crazy?"

"The word she used was babyish, but she only started in on that when I outgrew the jacket and she wanted to throw it out. I cried. I really cried over a stupid jacket."

"It wasn't stupid. It represented something you needed."

"It was a jacket, for God's sake, a cheap little jacket! What kind of kid has a love affair with a jacket? Anyway, I made such a stink about the thing that not only did she steal it away from me and have it burned, but she made sure that the next jacket she bought had no fur on it. It was an abrasive woolen thing. I hated it. I hated her."

"You didn't really."

"I did really," he stated with such calmness that Paige almost believed him. "She made my life miserable. It was like she had to constantly punish me for my existence. I felt totally alone in the world."

"But you had your brother, for a time at least. Didn't that help?"

"It was a different situation for my brother. His father may never have been around, but at least he sent gifts from time to time and money for clothes. Brian could dream that someone cared. I didn't have even that luxury."

Again Paige wanted to say how sorry she was, but loathe to rile him, she held her tongue. Her heart ached for the little boy who'd never known love, for the man who had steeled himself against that kind of vulnerability. She rubbed her cheek against his shoulder and tightened her arm about his waist, wanting nothing more than to give him that which he'd never had. But she wasn't his mother, and she couldn't make up for what he'd lost. And there was still more that she wanted to hear.

"How was it during your teenage years?"

"Better. My brother had left by then, but I was old enough to take care of myself so at least there weren't strangers pushing me around. I went to school with a key in my pocket. I came home to an empty house. When I got hungry I scrounged round for whatever happened to be in the refrigerator. My mother would usually stop in at dinnertime, then again around dawn. She was always sleeping when I got up in the morning, so it was no big thing when she didn't make it home some days. By the time I got to high school, I was the envy of every kid around. I was free-wheeling and independent, just like they wanted to be." He snorted. "They should have only known."

"Were you a good student?"

The snort was a dry laugh this time. "Not particularly. I resented authority. I still do, which is why my work suits me. I take jobs when I want. When I don't, I lie low."

"But you do work to please."

"That's the name of the game. This particular one, at least. I get in my shots, though. Believe me." He took a deep breath and his arms loosened. "I haven't seen my relatives for years and I don't care. So now you've heard *the* story. Fascinating, huh?"

What Paige felt just then wasn't fascination, it was frustration. She wanted him to keep holding her. She wanted to hug him back. But the moment was seeping away.

"It helps to explain lots of things," she said softly.

His arms fell away completely, until he was grasping the sides of the lounge chair. "What things?"

"Your view of the world. It's hard, y'know."

"Damned right, it's hard!" he boomed, dragging his arm from under her and quickly rising. "That's a mean world out there." He stalked to the edge of the deck.

Behind him, Paige sat up. "You've said that before, but I don't agree with you."

"Why should you? You've had it easy. You were never twelve and sick and struggling to clean up the mess you'd made when you'd thrown up all over the floor!" He whirled around, every muscle tense. "Do you have any idea what that's like, Paige? You're burning up with fever, your entire body is shaking, you're scared 'cause you feel like you're dying . . . and you feel guilty, guilty for the whole thing!"

She quickly rose and went to him. "No, Jesse, I've never had that experience, but that doesn't mean I can't imagine how horrible it must have been. It doesn't have to be that way, though. Your situation was unique—"

"Like hell it was! I've seen similar things time and again in the course of my work!"

"All right. Not unique. But one-sided. There's another side, the side I saw, the side you can just as easily have now if you choose to."

His tone grew stony. "What are you talking about?"

"Happiness. Security, warmth, comfort. Just because you didn't have those things as a child doesn't mean that they're not yours for the taking. You opt for the role of the cynic, you choose to see the negative side of life. You surround yourself with it, almost as if you want reassurance that there's no point in taking a risk for anything else. And that's where I disagree. All those good things are out there right alongside the bad. It's a matter of ambition. As long as you tell yourself that the world's a crummy place, you're content to live with the crumbs. On the other hand, if you dare to strive for something better, you might be surprised just how attainable that something better might be."

Jesse stared at her, eyes dark in anger. "I don't believe this discussion. Have you become a preacher now, Paige, a sermonizer? Or a psychologist bent on straightening my crooked outlook?"

"No."

"Then what?" he growled, hands in fists by his sides. "What's the point of all this? Here I tell you things I've never told another person, and you turn them on me."

"I'm not turning anything on you," she argued, trying to keep her voice steady. He was slipping away, slipping away. She felt helpless and inept. "I'm saying that I'm sorry you had to live with what you did for all those years, but that the scars won't fade unless you turn them to the sun."

He raked a hand through his hair. "God save me from the poetic mind. That I can very *well* live without."

"Then maybe you'd better leave," she stated quietly, "because I'm not about to change. You know, there are many people who have *everything*, but who keep themselves miserable wondering whether it's going to last. They become paranoid and suspicious. They're afraid to spend a dime for fear something's going to happen to the rest of their wealth. Well," she said angrily, "that may be their choice, but it's not mine. I refuse to sit here worrying about a day something terrible may happen. The odds are against me. No one goes through life without a little heartache. But I choose to be positive. It's the only way I can be."

When Jesse continued to stare at her through the darkness that now surrounded them, she badgered. "Well, haven't you got a retort?"

"I think you covered just about everything," he gritted.

If she'd hoped to impress him with what she'd said, it appeared that she'd failed. But then, she *wasn't* a psychologist, and even if she were she sensed it would take days, weeks, months to help him work through his anger. For it was anger. Masked behind cynicism, perhaps couched in bitterness, it was anger nonetheless. Anger at the mother who didn't care, at the father who hadn't been around, at the brother who had that little bit more and took the first road out, at the world that had allowed it all to happen.

He was missing so much in life that she wanted to cry for him. And after that, she mused, she'd cry for herself. Because she was falling in love with him. And it seemed hopeless.

Knowing that tears would do neither of them any good, she turned to leave. Her shoulders were hunched, her limbs weary. "I'm going in," she murmured sadly as she walked toward the house.

She hadn't expected him to follow, and he didn't. For a long, long time she lay in bed with an unopened book, wishing he'd come back fighting if for no other reason than to give her another shot. But he wouldn't. By choice he was a man alone in the world. All along he'd told her what to expect; she'd had no idea then how hard accepting that might be.

It was very late when he finally came to bed. Paige was still awake, wondering if he'd ever come, if perhaps he'd follow the suggestion she'd so blithely made that he leave. When she heard the rustle of clothing, she held her breath. He might be packing, in which case she had no one but herself to blame. The past two weeks had been almost idyllic; she should have left well enough alone.

Moments later he slipped under the covers, and she felt weak with relief. Oh, he'd leave sometime; she was sure of it. But each additional day would be another to treasure. She wasn't ready to lose him yet.

Jesse lay quietly for a time, staring at the ceiling. He was hurting her. He'd known he would, but he couldn't help himself. He also knew that he should leave, but that seemed somehow impossible, too. He was selfish, wanting one more day, always one more day. It stunned him that he continued to find her company so pleasant—barring, of course, the discussion they'd just had. Even now he wasn't quite sure how that talk had gotten out of hand. Even now he wasn't quite sure why he'd told her all those things. Perhaps it had been because she'd asked, or because she had shared so much of herself with him. Perhaps, just perhaps, he'd needed to voice it all after living so long with it buried inside. Why, then, did he feel an even greater burden on his shoulders? If he'd been counting on her to simply listen and accept, he'd miscalculated once again. Come to think of it, she'd done a similar thing the night that she'd first conned him into staying here. She'd parried his arguments—half-baked as even he knew they were—with aplomb, speaking up to him, expressing her opinions with eloquence. She wasn't a yes-person, not by a long shot, and the way she could so calmly and quietly inject her personal feelings into a discussion fascinated him. As always, she seemed so very sure of herself. It was enough to make a man wonder.

Turning his head on the pillow, he saw that her eyes were open. Looking at him in...fear? He began to ache.

"Paige?" he whispered. She blinked. "You okay?" She bobbed her head twice. "What are you thinking?"

She didn't say anything for a minute and when she did it was in a barely audible whisper. "I feel cold."

He groaned and turned to her. "Come 'ere." Sliding an arm under her, he pulled her to his warmth. She was as naked as he and, he sensed, as disinclined to make love. Something else was needed after what they'd just been through. Closeness. Simple, comforting closeness.

He heard her let out a breath and felt her snuggle even closer. She draped an arm around his ribs and burrowed her hand between his body and the sheet. Strangely, he didn't mind the gentle shackle, or the blanket of her hair on his chest, or the gentle weight of her leg over his. Rather, he found it all reassuring.

The last image that flitted through his mind moments before he fell asleep was of the soft jacket that had been his lone friend long ago.

6

WHEN THEY AWOKE the next morning, neither Jesse nor
Paige made reference to the discussion they'd had the
night before. In unspoken agreement they resumed the
pattern they'd established over the past two weeks.
Paige spent the morning working, stopping to breakfast with Jesse at ten before returning to her studio to
sculpt until midafternoon. He did any chores that
needed to be done, ran any errands, then relaxed, sitting down with a book, perhaps lying out on the deck
in the sun.

Outwardly things were the same. They talked softly
with each other, smiled, joked. Each new day brought
something new to admire; Paige found herself increasingly enthralled with Jesse and, since he made no move
to return to New York, she assumed that at least he
wasn't bored.

But there was something else now, something that
had taken root in that heartrending talk they'd had and
was a tiny ripple marring an otherwise smooth sea. It
was subtle, very subtle, a fine undercurrent of tension
that appeared from time to time in a look, a glance, a
stare. On Jesse's part, it came from an effort to understand just what it was about Paige that kept him here.
On her part, it stemmed from an attempt to cope with
her growing love.

Increasingly Jesse found himself deep in thought on the beach, tossing pebbles across the water in frustration. He'd never known a woman like Paige, one as poised and undemanding. But those very qualities, he found, could be unbelievably demanding.

Increasingly Paige found herself staring blindly at the work in her lap, seeing varying images of Jesse's face. Sometimes he was calm and absorbed, and intelligence marked his features. Sometimes he was angry, and his eyes darkened to midnight blue, the bridge of his nose tensed, his lips thinned. Sometimes he was gentle, and his gaze worshiped her and his concern for her well-being was boundless. And sometimes he was vulnerable.

The last didn't happen often. He seemed forever on his guard, as though he regretted having told her about his childhood and didn't want to make the same mistake twice. He saw himself as being strong, self-contained, she realized, and he'd actually been ashamed by the show of emotion he'd let slip out that night.

One thing Paige knew with growing sureness as the days passed. Jesse Dallas, for all his proclamations to the contrary, was a sensitive man. Just as he'd anticipated her needs that long hot day in New York, so he continued to do here. He'd materialize behind her in the studio just when her shoulders were beginning to ache and he'd massage them in silence until her energy returned. When he sensed she was tired he'd suggest an early night. He knew just when she'd had enough of one activity or another.

He was sensitive, too, in what he felt himself, though this he diligently sought to deny. Nonetheless Paige had seen the moistness in his eyes when he'd been reading a particularly moving piece of nonfiction, and she knew the pain he felt for the underprivileged of the world. She'd seen the way he took to the locals, inquiring with concern about the fisherman who'd broken his leg and was relegated to mind the dock. She'd seen the way he stopped to shoot baskets with a group of children on a local basketball court. On one such occasion he even ran up and down the court with a delighted six-year-old in his arms, letting the child slam-dunk his share to the playful chagrin of their opponents. And she'd seen the way he reached for *her*, seeking comfort from time to time.

For a man who was supposedly hard and callous, he had a remarkable capacity for warmth. Paige wondered if he'd always been that way, or if the past weeks had done something to release what had lain dormant all along. She knew that he'd never been anything but gentle with her. Oh, yes, they argued at times and he scowled and snapped and said things that hurt. But in the wake of such incidents he was all the more solicitous and caring. If she didn't know better, she might suspect he was falling in love with her.

She did know better, however. Rather, she knew she'd be foolish to read something into his softer side. He'd set out his terms at the start: no strings, no promises, no future. She had agreed; she did agree. After all, she'd been alone for years and she liked her life. The only thing she couldn't quite reason away was the chill she felt at the thought, the knowledge, that one day he'd be gone.

IT DIDN'T GET EASIER as the days passed. Despite the intense concentration that seemed to absorb more and more of Jesse's private time, there were light moments to share, moments when it seemed that they were made for each other, moments when their inevitable parting seemed absurd.

One morning, a drizzly day when outside activity was of necessity put on hold, Paige sat perched on a kitchen stool talking to her mother on the phone. She'd told her about Jesse the previous week, that she'd met him in New York and that he was spending his vacation at her home. When her mother had asked detailed questions about him—as mothers from tight-knit homes were wont to do—Paige had answered as many as she'd felt were pertinent and had deftly fielded the rest.

As it stood, her mother knew Paige liked the man; the simple fact that he was there was proof of that. Paige had never dated any man for long or with much interest, let alone invited him to share her home. Laura Mattheson knew that her daughter enjoyed living where she did, as she did. She also knew that, at twenty-nine years of age, Paige had a right to live with a man if she so chose, and though she might worry about her only daughter's future, she could only interfere so much.

So it was that on this particular day they were discussing not Jesse or the nature of Paige's feelings for him, but the upcoming annual golf tournament that was the highlight of Paige's father's summer.

"Is Daddy all set?"

"He's been on the course every afternoon for the past two weeks. I should hope he's all set. Funny, when he was working full-time in the city, I used to dream about the day when he'd retire and we'd have more time to spend together." She sighed wistfully across the telephone line. "Well, he's semiretired now and he's *still* gone all day. A woman can't win, it seems."

"Don't give me that, Mother," Paige chided with a smile, looking up to find Jesse coming to lean against the kitchen arch. Her smile broadened to one of welcome. "You were never one to be idle for long. You're still playing bridge twice a week, aren't you?"

"Of course. The girls send their best, by the way. Elizabeth's daughter had another baby. A girl this time, or have I already told you?"

"No, you haven't," Paige teased, arcing a mischievous look toward Jesse, who had left his post and was slinking toward the counter on which she rested her elbow. "How many grandchildren is it for Liz now?"

There was a running competition between the bridge friends to see who had the greatest number of grandchildren. For a time Laura had all but pleaded with her daughter to help out her side—among Paige's three brothers, the Mattheson tally was at five—but she'd long since learned that such pleading fell on deaf ears.

"Seven," Laura moaned. "She's not quite up to Vivie's eight, but she's getting there."

"Vivie has five children of her own," Paige replied. "Seems to me that's a distinct advantage. Shouldn't there be handicaps given in this thing like there are in golf?" When Jesse arched his brows, questioning the content of the conversation, she simply winked at him. This particular discussion he didn't need to hear; it'd make him nervous indeed.

"Handicaps!" Laura's voice brightened, as though she was actually considering the possibility. "That's not a bad idea. I'll have to mention it to the girls. Did I tell you about the garden-club meeting we had the other day?"

"No..."

Jesse was twisting a lock of Paige's hair around his finger, tugging gently from time to time. It wasn't the tugging she minded. It was the way his thumb brushed her neck. And "minded" wasn't really the word. It was more a matter of being distracted.

"It was marvelous!" Laura went on, unaware of her daughter's momentary preoccupation. "The fellow who spoke to us is one of the foremost iris breeders in the country."

"Iris breeders," Paige repeated. Jesse had pushed aside her hair and, leaning around her, was nibbling at her nape. His lips were warm, the moistness from his tongue cooling where the air then passed. She shivered, trying to concentrate on what her mother was saying.

"He's introduced the most amazing iris hybrids. He brought slides and as many plants with him as he could. They were beautiful. Coral and lime and..."

Paige sucked in her breath, then bit her lip to contain her delight when Jesse's mouth slid around to her collarbone. His fingers were paving the way, parting her shirt, brushing her skin in a manner that was seductive to say the least.

"Velvety texture in addition to being larger and richer in color," Laura rambled. "Unfortunately the newest things he's done won't reveal themselves in bloom for another three years. I told your father about them, and he said I should give the fellow a call. We're thinking of enlarging the greenhouse and . . ."

Paige's free arm now curved around Jesse's broad back. Her blouse lay open, mysteriously unbuttoned, and Jesse's lips were at her breast, setting fire to her swelling flesh. Moments later, his tongue dabbed sweet moisture on her nipple with devastating effect. She closed her eyes and let her head fall back. The hand that clutched the phone seemed to contain the only strength in her body.

Her mother's voice came at her from a distance. "I've already called the caterers and . . ."

Greenhouse . . . caterers . . . Through a haze Paige realized that she'd missed something. Clutching at Jesse's shoulder to hold him away, she lowered her head and muffled the phone against her neck. "Please, Jesse," she whispered frantically. "I can't follow what she's saying!" Returning the phone to her mouth, she managed a slightly shaky "Uh-huh" at what she thought might be an appropriate spot.

Jesse grinned and proceeded to slip a hand between her legs. She squeezed them together, succeeding only in heightening the red-hot sensation.

"Not that they weren't well recommended," her mother continued buoyantly, "but the salmon had bones and your father didn't think that there were enough hors d'oeuvres. So this time we'll try Georgia's people. She's been raving about them, and I do want this party to be a success." She paused, then went on, apparently not hearing the change in Paige's breathing. "Do you think you'll be able to make it, dear? Everyone wants to see you, and I'd love to be able to show you off."

An answer. Her mother wanted an answer. Paige tried to remember the question, but it was difficult with Jesse's hand stroking her that way. Something about a party, she thought, but when?

Taking a handful of Jesse's hair, she tugged sharply. Much as she adored what he was doing, she needed a breather long enough for her to end the conversion and get off the phone.

Dazed as her senses were by smoldering desire, she misjudged the force she used. Jesse yelped. Paige winced in silent apology. And Laura Mattheson finally caught wind of something happening.

"Paige, darling, what was that?" she asked cautiously.

"That? Oh, uh, that was Jesse, Mom. He's having trouble with something. I think I'd better give him a hand. Can I call you back another time? You'll give my love to Daddy, won't you?"

"Of course . . . to both," Laura said, seeming to accept Paige's hurried explanation and departure. "Take care, dear. I love you."

"Love you too, Mom," Paige said more quietly, feeling strangely sensitive about Jesse's overhearing those particular words. Bridge groups and garden clubs and caterers were one thing. But those last few words represented, in a nutshell, all he'd needed and had never had.

Straining forward to replace the receiver on its hook, she was hampered by the tight press of Jesse's face to her chest. She wondered if they'd bothered him, those words, and, wanting to comfort him, she began to stroke his hair.

"What did your mother have to say?" His voice was muffled, its tone almost indistinguishable.

"I don't know," she murmured. "I couldn't concentrate 'cause some sexy guy was making love to me. On the other hand—" she feigned a frown "—it might have been a bad connection. The weather's pretty lousy—"

Her teasing was cut off by a deep growl accompanied by hands sinking into her bottom, lifting her off the stool as Jesse stood. Whatever he intended to do, though, was put off by the ring of the phone.

"Not again," he moaned.

"Still. She's probably forgotten something she feels is positively urgent." Paige reached for the phone, fully expecting her mother to be on the other end of the line. "Hello?" she said in a singsong tone.

"Is this the Mattheson residence?" asked a male voice she didn't recognize.

She straightened, laying a restraining hand on Jesse's arm. "Yes."

"This is Benjamin Waite. I'm a friend of Jesse Dallas."

She recognized the name. Indeed so. "Yes?"

"I was told I might find him there."

She paused. "You might." As a matter of pride, she had no intention of making things easy.

"Is he, uh, available?"

She hesitated. "Yes."

"Can you call him to the phone?"

She waited. "Possibly." She was beginning to feel pleased with herself. The thought of that bet and the macho smugness that had been behind it challenged her to some form of retaliation.

"Uh . . . would you?"

This time she let him sit for a full five seconds. "If you say 'please.'"

Jesse, who'd been observing the one-sided exchange with a look of puzzlement, put his ear to hers in hopes of recognizing a voice. What he heard was a long pause, then an indulgent "Please?" in a voice he did, indeed, know well. With a chuckle, he took the phone from Paige.

"The woman's got this thing about our little bet, Ben," he began without preliminary, his eyes on Paige. "I think she was offended."

Page raised both brows and pointed to herself in an innocent who-me gesture. Then she slid her hands around his neck and, standing on her toes, touched the tip of her tongue to his free ear. Her retaliation had just begun.

"Not so offended that she hasn't forgiven you, it appears," Ben remarked, unaware of the shudder that shook his friend. "Or is she holding you hostage up there? Man, I was beginning to wonder when I didn't hear from you. There was no answer at your place, aside from that asinine machine of yours. I know your message by heart, I called so many times."

"Touching, Ben," Jesse murmured. When Paige lightly nipped his earlobe, he cleared his throat. "You called John?" His agent was the only one who'd known where he was. They'd talked on the phone several times in the past weeks; though Jesse wasn't ready to work, he wanted his options open.

"Yeah, and he wasn't thrilled about passing on the number."

"Confidentiality. It makes him feel important." If there was a husky timbre to Jesse's voice, it had nothing to do with the sarcasm of his words. Paige had lowered her hands and was tracing large circles on his chest. When he sent her a warning glance, she simply shifted tactics, using strategically placed thumbs as center points for the tracings.

"Whatever. Speaking of our bet, I take it you won."

"Yup," Jesse said, though again he wondered. To win implied dominance. Yet at that moment Paige seemed fully in charge.

"But you missed the play-offs."

"That's okay. I had better things to do." If he couldn't beat her, he'd have to join her. Slipping his hand around her, he ran his fingers slowly down her spine. She leaned forward and pressed an openmouthed kiss to his freshly shaved jaw while her hands began a descent of their own.

"Tell me she's teaching you to sculpt."

He cleared his throat again. "Not exactly."

"Then she's a great cook."

Her hands had reached the buckle of his belt. He felt like butter in a hot frying pan. Great cook? "Among other things."

Ben chuckled. "You must be mellowing, Jess. All this time with one woman. Are you sure you're feeling okay?"

"Feeling okay?" he echoed in a somewhat strangled tone. Having released the buckle of his belt, Paige had lowered his zipper and was in the process of invading his briefs. "Uh, I'm fine. Just fine." He closed his eyes and swayed, completely forgetting that he was supposed to be doing his share of the petting. He clutched Paige's hip, but only to support himself. His blood raced; his muscles twitched. It was always like this, this instantaneous desire. Paige's nearness was a potent aphrodisiac. Either that, or he'd taught her too well, he mused in a moment's lucidity. But Ben had said something else.

"Hmm?"

"Uh, forget it. Why is it I get the feeling that I'm interrupting something?"

Ben was a bit more astute than Paige's mother had been, but then he was a man, and he also knew Jesse well. Jesse grinned and mustered the strength to deliver the longest sentence he had to date in the conversation. Of course, his voice wasn't smooth; his breathing had grown suspiciously choppy. "You will be if . . . you keep me on much longer. Unless, of course, you . . . get your kicks listening to the sounds of—"

"No way," Ben asserted quickly. It was bad enough that Jesse Dallas got any woman he wanted, but to rub salt in the wound? "I'm going. Glad to hear you're okay, though. Any idea when you'll be back?"

"Uh . . . can't answer that right now." He burst out laughing, knowing it was a choice between that or screeching. The situation was truly ludicrous. How Paige expected him to think straight when she was rubbing him that way, he didn't know. But then, she'd gotten him back, hadn't she? He had to hand it to her. When it came down to it, his laugh was as much in pride and delight as in anything else.

"I read you loud and clear," Ben announced. "Listen, Jess, take it easy. You're not a kid anymore."

"Thanks," Jesse growled, but the growl was directed at Paige, who'd sunk to her knees and was about to . . . "I gotta go. Talk with ya later. 'Bye."

From that day on, it became a joke with them. When one was on the phone, the other played the distracter. It was as though neither wanted the interruptions that would remind them of the world beyond.

MANY OF THEIR lightest moments took place on the beach. When the sun was hot they played in the surf, splashing and dodging each other, drifting apart only to meet again atop a cresting wave. Paige discovered that Jesse was not only a powerful swimmer, he also— incidentally, of course—did marvelous things for the otherwise shapeless lycra nothing he wore. His body, lightly bronzed when she'd first met him, had taken on a deep golden hue from the time he'd spent in the sun. His sandy hair had grown lighter; the soft hair on his arms, legs and chest positively glowed. He was the embodiment of health and the source of a constant attraction for Paige.

One afternoon Paige stood in the shallows, watching Jesse stroke smoothly away from shore, turn and swim back. His arms arced with graceful strength, and sunlight sparkled on his wet flesh. When he turned to swim out again, she was hit by an idea. Running quickly across the beach and up the steps to the house, she returned in time to see him emerge from the waves. Lifting her camera to her eye, she snapped one picture, then another as he approached.

"What are you doing?" he growled, scooping his towel from the sand as he advanced on her.

Click. Whir. Click. "Capturing Poseidon."

"Poseidon, huh?"

"Yup." Click. From his waist up. Whir. Click. Head and shoulders.

"Is this another one of your talents?"

"Talents? I don't know." Click. Head only. He was directly before her. She lowered the camera and met his gaze. His hair dripped wetly on his forehead. His skin gleamed. "I've been known to take pictures of things I want to sculpt. I'm surprised I didn't think of this sooner."

He mopped his face, then his hair. "Come on, Paige. You're not on to that again, are you?"

"Sculpting you? Why not?

The towel seesawed around his neck. "Because my body's private, remember? And besides, I thought you were working on something else."

Having finished the grouping of sandpipers, she had indeed begun on a new piece. It was of limestone and she wasn't sure what it was—a new experience for her— but some compulsion kept her going. She was in the earliest stages of roughing out and was as fascinated by the shape taking form as she was mystified.

"I am, which is precisely why pictures of you might be nice. By the time I get around to doing anything with them, you might not be around. What would I use as a model then?"

Jesse's gaze grew harder. He was searching, she knew, trying to see if any emotion existed beneath her blithely worded explanation. She kept her expression light, but as he turned in silence and began to walk toward the steps, she had the sinking sensation that time was running out.

Deep down inside she wanted those pictures. To sculpt from, perhaps. To cherish, without a doubt. It was only a matter of days now before he'd be leaving. Every sign pointed that way.

In some respects, she felt as though she was living on borrowed time. She wasn't pregnant; she'd known that for nearly ten days. She'd half feared that Jesse would leave as soon as he knew. The fact that he hadn't was like a small gift, painful in its impermanence but precious nonetheless.

Wishing only to savor the gift while it lasted, she shouldered her camera and followed him up the steps.

PAIGE CONTINUED to photograph Jesse and, as much as he protested that he preferred being on the other side of the lens, he indulged her. It seemed a small thing, with so many larger ones on his mind.

With each passing day he grew more moody. Yes, he was getting the itch to work at last; he'd never taken a vacation quite as long as this. But what really bothered him was the fact that he felt so comfortable here.

Being with Paige day and night evoked emotions in him that he had neither the will nor the ability to handle.

Paige was aware that he was now in closer touch with his agent. She sensed his restlessness. When he began to spend more and more time on the beach, she respected his need for solitude and left him alone. Time and again she'd put down her work and walk to the glass wall of her studio to catch sight of his sandy hair, his downcast head as he walked the sand. And she knew that all she could do was to make things as warm, as comforting, as loving as she could for him when he returned.

Though she had the luxury of her work to keep her occupied, the occupation seemed more often than not limited to her hands alone, another reason why her new piece was a mystery. Her thoughts were still on Jesse. And though she told herself that the time she spent alone was good for her, that she'd better get used to solitude once more, doing so was harder than she'd ever dreamed.

BY THE TIME the seventh week approached, things had grown strained between them. The lighter times were fewer and far between. The inevitable seemed upon them.

It was Saturday. As she tried to do unless working on a deadline, Paige had steered clear of her studio. She'd slept late with Jesse and had made a hearty brunch. They'd driven to the small craft shops in Rockport and had returned. Silence had dominated the trip.

When Jesse suggested that they go out for dinner at one of the more elegant local restaurants, Paige had had a premonition of what was to come. When, dressed in their finery that night, they'd said more to the waiter than to each other, she'd known.

They'd returned to the house and were having brandy in the living room when she finally took the bull by the horns. "When are you leaving?" she asked quietly.

He glanced up from an intense study of the amber liquid in his snifter. There was neither surprise nor confusion on his face.

"Tomorrow." He held her gaze. "I'll be starting work on a new film on Monday."

Paige wondered how long he'd known, but knew that a show of indignation would do nothing but spoil their final hours together. She nodded. "What . . . uh, what is it on?"

"The CIA."

"Oh?"

He shrugged. "The CIA can be pretty depressing, but, yes, I think it'll be easier to take. The producer wants something that plays like an adventure. It might even be fun."

She smiled. "I'm glad." When he reached over and tugged at her shoulder, she slid the short distance on the sofa until she rested against him.

"You look pretty tonight," he said in the gruff tone she'd come to know so well but had missed in recent days.

Resting her hand on his thigh, she toyed with the crease of his trousers. "So do you."

"Pretty?"

"Handsome."

"Ah, that's better." Setting his snifter on the nearby table, he fingered the pearls that nestled in the vee of her teal-blue silk dress. "Very nice. You were made for pearls, or have I already told you that?"

Her skin warmed where he touched and she was suddenly overcome by the urge to throw herself into his arms and hold him until tomorrow passed. One more day she wanted. Then another. And another. Letting him go was going to be the hardest thing she'd ever done but, loving him as she did, she knew she had no choice. He was free, an adult. She couldn't hold him against his will. And evidently his will was to return to New York.

"Will you be okay?" he asked, suddenly sounding less sure of himself than she'd ever heard him sound. Where once she might have given an indignant retort, saying something to the effect that she'd lived alone for years and could very well do so again, she was struck by his concern and answered with it in mind.

"Sure. I'll be fine. You've fixed everything that needs to be fixed, so the house won't fall apart on me. I may even get some work done," she teased.

"You have been working."

"Not as much as usual. You're a distraction, or hadn't you noticed?"

"Then it's just as well that I'm leaving," he stated, grasping on the excuse as though it eased his guilt.

She tipped her head back and looked up at him. "I'll miss you, Jesse."

His eyes darkened, his voice grew more gruff. But he didn't push her away or stand up in a huff. Rather, his fingers tightened on her shoulder and he held her closer.

"Don't say that. I told you the day would come. I never planned to stay as long as this."

"I know. Why did you?"

"It's been . . . nice," he said more gently. "You're not bad for a roommate."

She saw the softening of his gaze and knew then that if they had one night left it would be a night to remember. Easing her own snifter to the floor, she put her hand to his face, tracing each of the features she now had indelibly etched both on film and in her mind. Well-shaped eyebrows, tiny crow's-feet at the corners of those soul-reaching blue eyes, lean cheeks faintly roughened by the beard that had begun growing the instant he'd shaved, a strong, firm jaw . . . she could touch forever and never tire.

"Neither are you . . . bad for a roommate," she breathed. "I'm surprised at how easy it was."

His gaze was touching her as her hand was touching him. The light in his eyes was warm, sad, intense. Catching her fingers, he drew them to his lips, taking one after another into his mouth, sucking gently on each. Rather than a gesture of studied seduction, it seemed one of need, a need that Paige was more than willing to meet. With fingers moist from his lips she brushed his cheeks, then leaned up and blew lightly on the streaks before wetting them again with her own tongue. She'd give him anything and everything he needed this night. That was what love was about, and she brimmed with it.

He kissed her then, lowering his lips to hers. What his mouth did, hers mirrored. The wetness of the open kiss only strengthened the bond.

Jesse pressed a long finger to her throbbing lips. "I'll take care of the glasses. Why don't you run ahead to the bathroom. I'll be right in."

"Let's do it here," she whispered, reluctant to let him go for an instant. But he was dragging her arms from his neck and pushing himself to his feet. He knelt for her glass and looked up at her.

"We're gonna do it right," he said hoarsely. "Long and thorough. For what I have in mind, this sofa is not the place."

The promise in his eyes set her blood racing in heated currents through her veins. She watched as Jesse stood, reached down and drew her to her feet.

"The bathroom?" he reminded her, a crooked smile on his face.

"The bathroom," she muttered, willing her knees to carry her there.

Moments later she stood before the open medicine chest, the small plastic case in her hand. She stared at it. The haze of passion lifted, and she stared harder. Slowly she opened it, then gazed at the rubber disk inside. Closing her eyes, she struggled to calculate the number of days it had been. A glimmer of excitement shot through her, accompanied by a sudden and intense determination that reflected a need as great as any she'd ever known. She opened her eyes to look once more at the disk, then carefully, quietly, closed the lid and replaced the case on the shelf.

The medicine chest snapped shut. She stood for a minute studying her reflection in the mirror. She put her hand on her stomach, moved it slowly downward over the silk of her dress. The trembling of her body intensified, but there was more than passion behind it. Knowing precisely what she was doing, she turned and left the bathroom.

Jesse stood in the bedroom, staring out at the ocean. Hearing the soft rustle of her dress, he turned. The look in his eyes was of a heated anticipation that had built even in the brief moments he'd spent waiting for her. His tie was unknotted and hung on either side of the center tab of his shirt. He'd released the top two buttons.

She was glad he was still clothed. She wanted to undress him. She wanted to slowly and carefully peel away his outer layers, to sculpt him and mold him, to forever embed in him the memory of who she was and what their time together had meant to her.

Closing the small distance between them, she looped her arms loosely around his neck. "You look like a god standing here," she whispered, smiling. "A very handsome god made of stone, who needs the touch of a mortal to bring him to life."

"Will you touch me?" he whispered back, too mesmerized by the look of adoration on her face to think seriously of its cause and rebel. Or perhaps he did know its cause but didn't care. Tonight he could be greedy. He'd be leaving tomorrow.

"Oh, yes," she murmured against his jaw. Her lids lowered and for a long moment she simply savored the musky scent that was his alone. "Mmm." She inhaled deeply. "So good."

She brushed her lips back and forth along his skin, its faint roughness heightening the sensations. Mouthing him softly, she slipped her hands under the shoulders of his blazer and pushed the fabric back and off his arms. Trailing her fingers back up those two strong limbs, she next went slowly to work at the buttons of his shirt. Anticipation quickened her breathing, and she reveled in the urgency she felt even as she restrained herself from rushing. Each step was beautiful. Each one she relished.

When his shirt was open, she pressed her face to his warm, hair-spattered flesh. Her hands charted the muscular swells, feeling his shudder, absorbing it with her lips.

"Dear God," he murmured. "I don't think I'm going to be able to take this."

"You'll take it," she whispered with confidence, but she began to ease the shirt from his shoulders. "You'll take it and more. You love it. Confess."

"I love it, I love it," was his hoarse chant as his hands guided her head in its tormentingly slow shift. The feel of her lips on his flesh was like fire. The dab of her tongue did little to quench the flame. He shifted his stance in an effort to steady his legs, but it seemed a losing battle.

Bare from the waist up, he submitted to her sensual manipulation. while her mouth was busy tasting and teasing every inch of his chest, her hands on his back were those of a sculptress. The tactile exploration took her over bunching muscles, into softer hollows. He was sure she'd separately identified each and every one of his vertebrae before she finally granted him a rest from the steady strain of desire that threatened to erupt violently.

"How do you feel?" she asked against his lips once more.

"I'm dying," he grated. "Dying. How can you do this to me, Paige?"

"How can I not?" was her whispered reply, and he understood and agreed and contained the urge to throw her on the floor and take her instantly.

Paige would have nothing to do with "instantly." Setting the pace as she was, she wanted everything to last. If her own body cried out for release—which it did vociferously—she had only to think of tomorrow night and the night after that, and she was in control once again. This night she'd remember, every tiny, tormentingly beautiful moment of it. She'd decided that. So it would be.

Their kisses reflected the duality of their desire, swinging from gentle to fierce and back to gentle, vacillating between the needs of the body and those of the mind. Lips caressed, teeth nipped, tongues repaired the damage only to fuel the hunger. The air was rent with tiny moans, from whose throat Paige neither knew nor cared. The attraction, the fascination, the fire was shared; that seemed all that mattered.

Closing her eyes and pressing her forehead to Jesse's chin, Paige took several long, ragged breaths.

"What's wrong?" he teased. "Trouble breathing?"

"No, no. Just trying to steady the pace."

"Of breathing . . . or loving?"

"Both," she murmured, knowing the truth of the confession. Her hands seemed glued to his shoulders, as though they wanted to remain forever. Of course, the support was a boon to her quaking knees.

"I could help you out," he offered gruffly. "I'm an expert at taking off my pants."

"I'm sure you are," she drawled, "but I can manage, thank you." Already her hands had moved to the buckle of his belt. She imagined she was wielding a new tool in the sculpting process, still trying to bare the surface of the stone on which she worked.

The belt was unbuckled. Her fingers brushed the firm skin of his belly, and releasing the catch of his trousers was made easier when he sucked in a breath. Catch unfastened. Zipper tab raised. She paused, rubbed her cheek against his breast, swirled her tongue around one dark areola. His nipple was erect; she basked in her success, then furthered it with the tip of her tongue. The ploy backfired when she found herself quivering in contact with the tight nub.

"Hurry...hurry..." Jesse rasped, arching his hips against her hand.

But she wouldn't hurry. She couldn't. If this night was to hold her a long, long time she had to make it last forever. And once a layer had been removed from the stone, it could never be replaced. She wanted to fully appreciate each new facet as it was revealed.

To the tune of the surf beyond the rocks, Jesse's zipper rasped slowly down. She slid her hands inside the plackets, then knelt to ease his trousers over his hips. In this he helped her, stepping out of his loafers so that both trousers and socks could go. When he stood before her wearing nothing but his briefs, she sat back on her heels to look at him. He'd done the same to her that first night. Only now could she appreciate what he'd felt then, an awareness of beauty so intense that her hands trembled at the thought of touching it. She felt awed by his power. In her eyes Jesse was perfection.

She steadied her fingers by curving them around his ankles, then moved them upward over calves that were sinewed and strong. Her hands ruffled hair as they moved, hair that exemplified masculinity in such a small but exciting way. His knees seemed thicker, as if locked in desperation. Corded muscles stood out on his thighs, hard to her touch, growing harder beneath it like living marble, rich and firm.

"You are a work of art," she breathed brokenly. "We sculptors think we have talent, but it's nothing compared to His."

"Religion now," came the low moan above her. "Oh, my God." But it wasn't criticism as much as sheer agony.

"Patience," she whispered as she slid both hands to the backs of his thighs, finding them strong and textured. When she leaned forward to bury her face against his leg, he clutched at her hair.

"I've run out, love! I want you undressed!"

"Me . . . undressed?" She was so enraptured by what she'd found beneath his clothes that she hadn't yet thought that far.

"That's how it's normally done," Jesse growled, grasping her under her arms and hauling her to her feet. When he began to hurriedly fumble with the back zipper of her dress, she stepped away. This time she was going to do it, she decided. Always before either he'd done it or they'd tugged at their clothes simultaneously. This time would be different. This time Jesse would know exactly how far she'd come from the innocent, near-virgin he'd first made love to so many weeks before.

There was nothing outwardly seductive in her movements as she unzipped the dress, slid it from her shoulders and let it fall in a pool at her feet. Her eyes didn't tease. Her hips didn't sway. Rather, her demeanor was one of conviction and love and, even in spite of the two, the faintest flicker of fear. She needed to please the godlike creature she adored, and no amount of self-possession could hide that need.

Heart thumping, she stepped out of her slip. Hands trembling, she reached back to release the catch of her bra, then eased the lacy confines from her breasts and dropped the wisp of material to the floor. Eyes on his as he closely followed her progress, she rolled down her panty hose and peeled them from her feet. When she stood perfectly naked, she waited for a sign of his approval. For as many times as they'd made love, she'd always needed that. Without it, her determination meant nothing.

He pressed his lips together. His collarbone stood out above wire-taut muscles. His eyes raked her figure with a slowness she'd have thought beyond him at that moment. Only when he met her gaze with eyes that positively smoldered did she feel free once more. Without words he conveyed his own adoration, then he met her hand when she reached out to draw him toward the bed.

With a flick of her wrist the cover was turned back. With a second flick, the blanket and top sheet joined it in a hillock at the foot of the bed. Jesse freed himself of his straining briefs, for just a moment stunning Paige with his ardor. Regaining control then, she urged him down, following with the same innocent sensuality with which she'd undressed.

She stretched out over him, letting her body take part in an exploration of his rugged form. She ran her foot up and down his leg. Her belly familiarized itself with the firmness of his. Her hands worked from his ribs to the concavity beneath his arms, finally propping themselves flat on the sheet as she rose to find his lips with her own.

It was a kiss made all the more heated by the intimate molding of their bodies. Her breasts swayed with every breath she took, nipples brushing against his until every pore, every nerve end had taken flame. Scorched, she drew back. There was work yet to be done—the fine shaping and polishing and finishing that would end in joyous conflagration for them both.

Straddling his legs, she knelt above him for a minute. His eyes were heavy lidded and smoky, his lips slightly parted to aid the labored working of his lungs.

"Paige . . ." he warned, his fingers sinking into the flesh above her elbows.

He was at the end of his tether, which was just where she wanted him to be. He was going to know what it was like to go nearly mad with want. He was going to know what it was like to be worshiped. He was going to know, once and for all, that there was no other woman, no other woman in the world for him. And he was going to know just how much she loved him, whether he liked it or not!

What took place then was something that Paige could never have consciously choreographed. Driven by the love she had to express, she touched and tasted every inch of his body, finding one part more precious than the next, treating each with fevered reverence. He was writhing, straining toward release when she finally rose and lowered herself onto him. At that moment, without severing their connection in any way, he rolled them over and took the dominant position.

It was only a position, for the dominance was shared. Who drove the other harder, who took the greater pleasure was something neither could determine even when they reached one apex and began a heady climb to the next. Paige only knew—much, much later, when neither could move a limb—that she had indeed found the secret of this stone. Hard though Jesse was on the outside, inside he was filled with love. He spoke it through his body, as Paige did through hers. He murmured it in broken thoughts when the frenzy of passion stripped away that last flimsy layer that shielded his soul. "Yes...oh, love...yes...sweet...I'm yours...dear heart...!"

He'd never have admitted it if she confronted him, so she didn't. But the next morning, when he determinedly packed his things and carried them to the car, the knowledge that for a tiny period of time he'd loved her fully was some comfort.

"Take care of yourself," he said quietly, pausing only to give her a final poignant look before climbing into the car and driving off.

Indeed she would take care of herself, because now she had a secret of her own. With a conviction that was uncanny but very, very real, she knew she was pregnant.

7

THE FIRST THING Paige did after Jesse left was to take a huge wad of clay from the storage closet, raise it high above her head and ram it mercilessly against the workbench surface. Over and over she did it, pounding the clay from time to time with her fists before lifting it and slamming it down again. Only when her arms were weak from exertion did she stop and sink onto the nearby stool. Her body was tired, but her heart was heavy as stone. When she finally mustered the will to move, she wandered to the beach, where she sat for hours. She stared at the sea, choosing a distant wave, following it in to shore. She looked at the sky and wondered that its blueness could be so vital while her own blue mood was a leaden weight. She searched the sand for Jesse's footprints, but if there had been evidence of his presence once upon a time, the tide had washed it away.

When the heat of the sun began to prickle her skin, she returned to the house to drift aimlessly from room to room. Quiet pierced her ears. Emptiness filled her view. She felt suddenly and strangely alone . . . and she grew slowly furious. Her life had been fine, just fine before he'd entered it! She'd *loved* silence, *thrived* on solitude. She hadn't needed *anyone*, much less a man, to liven up the day. But that had changed . . . thanks to Jesse Dallas.

Back in her studio again, she wielded the clay a while longer, lifting it high, slamming it down, relentlessly pommeling it with her hands. If this was a temper tantrum, she was loving every minute of it. Loving it . . . hating it . . . suffering inside as though a vital part of her had been cut out and skewered.

When exhaustion took over, she turned her back on the studio and, trailing to the living room, collapsed on the sofa. She dozed; she awoke. Time held little meaning. She lay listlessly out on the deck. She walked the beach again. The sun had begun to lower in the western sky before she realized she hadn't eaten since breakfast. With little enthusiasm she managed to down half a sandwich and a glass of milk, but the sandwich might have been paste, the milk dishwater.

Picking up the book she'd started several days before, she sat on the sofa and tried to read, but her stomach kept knotting and, before long, she sought solace in bed, in the sweet oblivion of sleep. It eluded her for long hours. She tossed and turned, then jumped up, stripped the bed and put on fresh sheets. She'd be damned if she'd have to smell him, too! It was bad enough that she could see him, an ever-present vision wherever she went. Damn him! Damn her own vulnerable heart!

It was long into the night before she finally fell asleep. When she awoke the next morning, she felt vaguely disoriented. Groggily she blinked, then rolled to her side. The other half of the bed was perfectly neat, the pillow as fully fluffed as it had been the night before.

Slowly, inevitably, reality set in. She lay board still, fingers clenched into fists by her mouth. Her pulse grew erratic, as though something was squeezing her heart, squeezing and twisting and causing the most excruciating pain.

Then she began to cry.

Tears fell full and fast from her eyes. Soft, soulful sobs slipped through her lips. She curled into a ball, hugging the pillow for comfort, and cried. And cried. Everything she'd done the day before had been for the frustration, the anger, the loneliness she'd felt; this was for the sorrow.

She loved Jesse Dallas with all her heart. Now he was gone. He hadn't called the night before; she hadn't expected him to. The break had been made and made cleanly. She was simply going to have to adjust.

Wiping the tears from her eyes, she sat up cross-legged on the bed. As minutes passed, her head cleared. Though her limbs still trembled, she knew they'd calm in time.

Determination was an antidote, spreading slowly through her veins, giving her strength. She'd adjust. Oh, yes! She'd resume her life as it had been before *he'd* stepped into it. She'd sculpt. She'd eat, sleep, walk, read, see her friends from time to time. She'd forget that Jesse Dallas had ever been—no, no, she wouldn't do that. She loved him; she'd always love him. And besides, microscopic though it yet was, she had his baby. No, she'd never forget him. She didn't want to forget him. What they'd shared had been too beautiful for words. These memories, plus her own maternal instinct, would guarantee that their child would be born and raised with love.

Placing her hand low on her abdomen, she studied it resting there. A miracle? Love was the miracle. To have a child who embodied that love would be her salvation.

Sitting straighter, she raised her head. Then slowly, her lips curved into the softest, most serene of smiles, and she was ready to face the future once more.

IT WASN'T AN EASY ROAD at the start. Paige went through the motions of normal living, doing all the things she'd done before. But she was repeatedly stunned by how much she missed Jesse. The house didn't seem the same. The outings she took were somehow lacking. The evenings were thunderously quiet. And, of course, there were the cravings. She had only to picture him standing before her and her body began to tingle. The tingle grew to a tremble, then an ache. She ached, damn it, she ached. And there wasn't a thing she could do about it!

Jesse Dallas, whether he'd known it or not, had chipped through the complacency of her existence, finding holes she hadn't known were there, needs she'd prided herself on being above. If they were flaws, she could find no fault with them. Ever the sculptress, she was simply going to have to work around them, to use them to her benefit. It was a challenging project. Jesse had added a new dimension to her life; it would take every bit of her skill and determination to compensate for its loss.

There were times when she was angry or frustrated or hurt, but those times grew fewer, each less intense than the one before. By the end of the first month, she was comfortably back in the routine she'd established before her fateful trip to New York.

Work was her major solace and she poured herself into it heart and soul. The piece she'd started before Jesse had left took shape as a child in the early stages of uterine development. It frightened her at times that she'd begun it even before she'd decided she wanted a baby. She wondered if it reflected a maternal instinct she'd subconsciously harbored for some time, or whether the womanhood that had blossomed under Jesse's caring hand had spawned it. Whatever the case, she took great pleasure in sculpting the small fetally tucked form. There was a liquidity to its shape suggestive of its suspension in amniotic fluid, but there was a realism as well in tiny features—eyelids, ears, mouth. Lifelike fingers and toes emerged from the swirling mass much as had Jesse's fingers from the stone she'd picked up on the beach. Whereas then the fingers she'd sculpted had been masculine, those she did now held the fragility, the innocence of the not-yet-born. When she finished the piece, she found herself thoroughly in love with it. But a mother raised her child to let it go one day, didn't she? It was with reluctance and great, great discipline that she gently crated the stone and sent it off to New York.

She began work on a second piece, this a dancer carved from a piece of yew that she'd let age in her storeroom for just the right amount of time. As she sculpted carefully and with due concentration, the heat of August abated and September came.

Her pregnancy was now fact. She didn't need a doctor's confirmation, so firm had been her conviction from the start. Even had that not been so she couldn't have missed the ripening of her breasts, the shadowy appearance of tiny blue veins, the first subtle changes in her body.

Her joy was tempered only by the awful sickness that set in soon after, a nausea that was far from limited to mornings and prevented her from holding down much of anything she ate. At this point she did see her doctor, who assured her that she was in fine health and that what she was experiencing was perfectly normal for a woman who was six weeks pregnant. When she offered her medicine to control the nausea, Paige refused it, opting instead to follow her doctor's suggestion that she eat small amounts of easily digestible foods at frequent intervals throughout the day. This helped somewhat, though she still had bad moments when she craved nothing more than Jesse's warm, strong hand bracing her in her agony. But he wasn't there. She hadn't heard from him at all. And she had to be strong, if not for her own sake then for that of the child she carried. When she continued to lose weight and called the doctor in alarm, she eased her worries with a chuckle, telling her that soon enough she'd have the reverse complaint. Thus assured, Paige found the sickness easier to accept.

More than once she was grateful to the nature of her profession, which allowed her to take breaks when she needed, to lie down and rest when she felt tired, as she did increasingly. This, too, the doctor assured her would pass, so she didn't fight it and found herself napping regularly each afternoon.

More often than not, the evenings found her curled on the sofa buried in one of the books she'd picked up on pregnancy and childbirth. At these times she'd grow more excited than ever—excited and proud, a little bit frightened, and on occasion sad. She wanted Jesse to be sharing this with her. Miracles in his life had been nonexistent; it grieved her to know that he was missing one now. The knowledge that a baby was growing inside her, that one day it would be a living child to hold and nurture and love, was truly wondrous. As much as he might declare that he didn't want a child, she had a deep conviction that, even against his will, he'd treasure it. It was, after all, a child of his blood. That was the thought that gave her the greatest comfort during the nights that seemed so long.

The end of September found Paige packing her bags and heading for Connecticut. She was looking forward to seeing her family. The grand party that Laura Mattheson had been planning since June had given even her brothers an excuse to come home. When one's father reached a robust and healthy seventy, it was indeed cause for celebration.

Paige's mother knew that Jesse had left. She'd been wonderfully gentle and supportive during those times when Paige had called, feeling down. Paige hadn't yet said a word about her pregnancy. She'd debated long and hard about how to break the news. Not that her parents wouldn't be overjoyed at the prospect of another grandchild, but...Paige wasn't married. For that reason word of her pregnancy might throw them. Wanting nothing to mar the long-planned celebration, she knew she'd have to carefully pick her time. Though her brothers and their families were leaving the day after the party, Paige had planned to stay on a bit longer. That was when she hoped an opportune moment might come.

It didn't quite work that way.

She arrived in Westport on Friday afternoon, with the party planned for Saturday night. Her mother was there to meet her at the door, as beautifully dressed and coiffed as ever, with an added excitement in her eyes.

"Paige!" Grinning broadly, she held out her arms and took her daughter into a fond embrace, which Paige returned with a force that surprised them both. Only at that moment did Paige realize how much she'd missed the warmth of human contact.

Loosening her arms with reluctance, Paige stood back for her mother's inevitable inspection. She'd dressed more carefully than ever, choosing sweater and slacks in coordinating shades of lavender, applying makeup to counteract the slimness of her face and the hollows beneath her eyes, waving her hair as softly as possible around temple and cheek.

Her efforts had been in vain, but then, a mother's eye was by nature keen. "You look tired," Laura said. Her quiet tone echoed the concern in her eyes.

"*You* look marvelous! I like your color."

Laura touched her hair, but Paige's attempt at diversion went no further. "Aren't you feeling well?"

"I'm fine."

"You're still upset by that fellow's leaving."

"His name is Jesse, and I'm, uh, I'm getting used to it."

Wrapping an arm around her daughter's shoulders, Laura led her into the house. Her eyes remained fixed, though, on Paige's face. "This will be a good vacation for you, then. I hope you've brought plenty of things. I thought we could go shopping one day next week. If you want to, that is." Her brows knit. "Are you sure you're not coming down with something?"

Coming *out* with something was more like it. "I'm sure. Is Daddy home?"

"He's gone to the airport to pick up Bill and Angie and the kids. Jason and Annette came in last night. They're at the club with Todd. He couldn't wait to see the pool. Michael and Sheila are driving down with the girls tomorrow morning."

Paige raised her eyes in a sweep around the large front hall of the elegant Tudor home. "This is the calm before the storm, then."

Laura chuckled. "You could say that. But we won't mind the storm a bit. It's too quiet around here most of the time. It's the nicest gift for your father—having you children here with us. It's not often that everyone can make it at the same time."

"This is a very special occasion. Is he looking forward to the party?"

"Yes, ma'am. Come. I'll make us some honey tea. That should put color in your cheeks."

"There is color in my cheeks."

"Artificial. Every speck. You might be able to fool the world, but you can't fool me, Paige Mattheson." They were on the kitchen threshold. "Do you want to go on upstairs while I heat the water?" Her voice took on a teasing note. She knew how much Paige enjoyed touching base after being away for a time. "Your room's waiting."

Paige grinned. "Then I'd better hurry. Rooms get very impatient." Giving her mother a quick peck on the cheek, she returned to the hall, grabbed her suitcase and started up the stairs.

Her room was the same as it had been when she'd left to go to college eleven years before. It wasn't the room of a child, or a teenager; Mattheson bedrooms had been redecorated with regularity as the children had passed from one stage to the next. Redone the summer before her senior year in high school, this room was that of a young woman. Bold florals dominated in shades of yellow and green and white. It was cheerful, but sophisticated, with French provincial furniture and just the right touch of softness.

Paige stood at its door feeling strangely melancholy. Stepping inside, she set down her bag, fingered the back of the scrolled chair by the dressing table, then approached the bed and brushed the quilt coverlet with her palm. Sliding one hip against the bed, she slowly lowered herself to its yielding surface.

She'd been happy in this room now filled with memories. These four walls had seen her playing with toys as an infant, going off to school for the first time, entertaining afternoon chums as pint-size as she in the days before homework had precluded such playtime. They'd overheard hours of inane chatter when, as a birthday gift in her thirteenth year, her parents had installed the Princess phone that lay quiet now on the nightstand.

She smiled, remembering her friends and the fanciful talks they'd had. They'd gossiped and giggled and dreamed, dreamed of husbands and of the children they'd have and the things *they'd* do differently. At the time, there was always pretense of one complaint or another, but Paige knew in her heart that she'd be lucky to give *her* child the very same things she'd had. If she was unable to give it a father, she'd simply have to compensate in other ways.

Taking a long, slightly unsteady breath, she lowered her eyes to her hands, determinedly placed them on the spread on either side of her and pushed herself up. Pausing only to brush her hair and dust an additional bit of color on her cheeks—though her mother might see through the ploy, her father and brothers were sure to be fooled—she headed back downstairs.

Laura was in the breakfast nook off the kitchen, stirring her tea with a spoon, deep in thought. At the sound of Paige's heels on the ceramic tile, she looked up.

"Millie's coming in for dinner," she said, feeling called upon to explain the housekeeper's absence. "She's looking forward to seeing you, but she wanted to spend a little time at home since she won't be taking Sunday off."

"How is she?"

"Remarkable, given the fact that she's sixty-five herself. Actually, it's worked out well. I don't need her full-time, what with all of you off and on your own, so when her arthritis is acting up she stays home. She's promised me, absolutely promised me that the arthritis will behave itself at least through Sunday. I thing she's as excited about the party as we are. She'll be in command of quite a fleet in here."

Smiling, Paige slid into the place Laura had set beside her own. Tea was steeping. A plate of small pastries, with crackers and cheese on the side, awaited her pleasure.

"Is everything set for tomorrow night?" Paige asked, reaching for a cracker nonchalantly. She was acutely aware of her mother's renewed scrutiny.

"I think so. The tent is being set up in the yard in the morning. The tables, chairs and linens should come soon after that. The florist promised me he'd be by at three. The caterers arrive at five. There's really not much that I have to do, other than have my hair and nails done and make sure the children don't play with the silverware once it's set out."

Paige gave a fond smile. "I can't wait to see them. I bet they've all grown."

"Mmm. Todd has. He's the most precocious five-year-old I've ever seen." Her expression of grandmotherly pride would have been complete had it not been for the slight worry crease between her eyes. "Have some cheese with the cracker, dear. It's fresh brie."

Paige's stomach tripped at the thought. She crinkled up her nose and reached for her tea. "Uh . . . I think I'll pass. Mmm. Sweet. Honey makes it, don't you think?"

Her mother was not thinking of honey, nor did she have any intention of doing so. "What's wrong, Paige? Something is, and you can deny it as much as you want, but you won't convince me. You're pale. You've got shadows under your eyes. And you've lost weight. If there's one thing you don't need, it's that."

Slowly setting down her cup, Paige looked at her mother. It was probably her biggest mistake, for the look of concern on Laura's face chipped at her resolve and she was beset by a wave of emotion. She'd wanted to wait, to have the party over and done with before chancing to say something that might or might not be upsetting. But this was her mother, and they'd always been close. Laura's next words did nothing to ease her dilemma.

"I'll worry until you tell me, darling," she said softly. "You know that. I'll imagine all kinds of horrible things."

"This is blackmail," Paige countered, forcing a smile that didn't quite make it.

"It's the truth. You look as though you've been ill. But there's something else." She paused, holding Paige's gaze. "Something in your eyes. I remember the time you came home from school with a look like that in your eyes. You'd been invited by your art teacher to go to an exhibit at the Guggenheim and, as excited as you were, you were terrified that we'd object."

Paige remembered. She gave her mother a rueful grin. "You did."

"But only until we learned that the teacher's wife was going along. He was young and attractive, that art teacher of yours. You were sixteen years old. It wouldn't have been proper for you to have gone with him alone."

It was all Paige could do to contain the hysterical laugh that threatened to bubble forth. If her mother had thought *that* would have been improper, she could imagine what the reaction would be to the current news. Needing to do something, she nibbled gingerly at her cracker, then wished she hadn't for her stomach was queasy.

"Mr. Antone was a newlywed, mother. He was in love with his wife. He only invited me because he knew how much I'd love the exhibit. Besides, even if his wife hadn't been along, if he'd done anything improper I'd have known how to take care of myself. I knew my way around the city. I'd have caught a cab to the train and come right home."

Laura's watchfulness was as intense as ever. "That's beside the point now, all in the past. Just that look in your eyes brought it back. It's . . . it's as though you've got something you're dying to tell me, but there's that . . . that little bit of fear." She put her hand over Paige's and squeezed gently. "You can tell me, darling. I'm strong. I can take it." The tiny hint of teasing took the edge off her concern, though the concern itself remained.

With a soft half laugh, Paige looked down. "You always did see too much. It wasn't fair, y'know. Every girl has a right to some secrets."

"I know *you*, darling. That's more than some parents can say of their children. And I loved you dearly. I still do." She lifted her hand to tuck a dark wave of hair behind Paige's ear. "Which is why I want you to tell me what's brought you here looking like you can't keep a thing in your stomach, much less get enough sleep."

Her choice of words had been strictly by chance, but something about their juxtaposition brought her to a halt. She glanced down at the half-eaten cracker on the saucer, then back at her daughter's face.

"You got it," Paige murmured.

"You're . . . pregnant?"

Despite the anxiety Paige felt in anticipation of her mother's reaction, she couldn't contain the soft smile that broke through on her lips. "Yup."

Laura's eyes widened. *"Pregnant?"*

"As in going to have a baby. Looks that way."

Laura straightened. "You can't be serious, Paige. I mean—" she began to sputter "—I mean, you're not married!"

"I know that."

"And you're pregnant." As though to deny it, she shook her head. Not a hair moved. "I thought your generation was expert at making sure this kind of thing didn't happen."

"We are. The techniques are all there and very efficient." She smirked. "It's when you don't use them that funny things like morning sickness occur."

"This is no time to be flip, Paige," her mother scolded. "You're an intelligent girl. I'd have thought you'd have done the wise thing."

"I did." There was not a trace of flippancy in her sober tone. "I chose to have a child."

"You *chose*? How could you *do* that when you're all alone?" She shook her head more slowly this time. "I don't think you've given this proper thought."

"Mother, even if that were true—which it isn't—it's not the issue. The issue is that I'm pregnant. It's a fact." She took a breath, then lowered her voice. "I can't believe you'd suggest I try to reverse it."

"Lord, no!" Laura exclaimed, her pallor growing more marked. "You can't kill that child. It's yours!"

Paige smile. "Yes, it is mine."

"And you want it, don't you?"

"More than anything. When I think of it getting bigger and bigger by the day, I get giddy."

"Then you throw up," Laura interjected wryly.

"The doctor says morning sickness is a good sign. Besides, it'll pass. You should know that. You had four children of your own."

"And a husband."

Paige sighed. "Things can't always be perfect. I've been pretty lucky so far. I have a career, a home and plenty of love to give a child." Her eyes softened almost beseechingly. "I really do want the baby, Mom. It's mine. Mine—" her voice caught "—and Jesse's."

"Jesse's gone," Laura stated unnecessarily. "Does he know?"

"No."

"But you're going to tell him, aren't you? Surely he'd marry you—"

"No, I'm not going to tell him. I haven't heard from him since the day he left. I was the one who wanted the baby. I never discussed it with him. And I have no intention of calling him with unfair expectations, *least* of all marriage. I don't want anything from him. I don't *need* anything from him . . ." Her voice dropped with her gaze. "At least not where the baby's concerned."

"But Paige—" Laura's head shot around at the sound of a horn and her expression grew worried. "Oh, dear, that'll be your father." She looked back at Paige even as she stood. "We'll talk more about this later."

Paige caught her hand as she started toward the door. Her eyes were wide, her voice clipped and urgent. "Don't tell Daddy. Not yet. I don't want him upset before the party."

"He ought to be told," Laura said in the quietly reproving voice she used when she felt her daughter should know better.

"He will be," Paige continued with the same urgency. "I'll tell him as soon as things have quieted down on Sunday. Please, Mom?"

Laura's mouth was pinched as she pondered that for a minute. "I suppose it could wait. I don't want him upset either. Okay, it'll be our secret until after the party. But you'll have to tell him then. The longer you wait, the more hurt he'll be."

Implied in her words was the knowledge that he'd be hurt as it was, and Paige felt the slightest bit guilty at having done something to disappoint him. Then she caught herself. She was an adult and she'd made a conscious decision, knowing what to expect, feeling confident that she could handle the consequences. Guilt was the last thing she should be feeling, particularly when at this moment she felt vaguely ill.

She mustered a weak smile and nodded. Laura stared at her a minute longer, then, squeezing her shoulder, left to welcome the homecoming troop. Paige took several minutes to steady herself before following in her wake.

THE REUNION was a joyous one, growing more so when Jason and family returned from the club and again the following morning when Michael and company arrived. From then on, the house was in a perpetual whirl. Paige threw herself into the festivities and was genuinely happy even in spite of the occasional worried glances sent her way by her mother. If she felt queasy from time to time, the excitement diverted her mind from her discomfort. She was careful of what she ate, determined to pamper her stomach and avoid what she was sure would cause awkward repercussions.

Her father was so thrilled to see her that he overlooked those things that her mother had noticed from the start. With his children and grandchildren gathered around him, he was in his glory. With the addition of a multitude of friends and business associates on Saturday night, he was aglow. Paige shared his excitement with a pride of her own. The enthusiastic gathering was a testament to her father's affability and the high respect in which he was held.

In every respect the party was an overwhelming success. The caterers were gone by midnight, the musicians by one. It was nearly two in the morning before the last of the guests had departed, nearly three before the Matthesons themselves finally went to bed. And it was almost noon on Sunday before Laura crept quietly into Paige's room, sat down on the edge of the bed and gently shook her sleeping daughter's shoulder.

"Paige?" she whispered, then raised her voice a notch. "Darling, it's almost noon." When Paige turned her head on the pillow and sighed, obviously still asleep, Laura shook her shoulder again. "Time to get up, Paige. Paige?"

Opening first one eye then the other, Paige frowned and looked hazily around the room. "Mother," she finally managed through a dry throat. She moaned and turned onto her side, pulling her knees up tight. "What time is it?"

"Almost noon," Laura repeated patiently. "You'd better get up soon or you'll miss brunch completely."

Paige forced her lids wider. "Brunch?" Moaning again, she wrapped her arms around her stomach. Even the word was distasteful to her. "How can anyone think of eating after last night?"

Laura grinned. "The children demanded breakfast at eight. This will be their lunch."

"Breakfast . . . lunch . . . how can you do this to me, Mother?"

Laura's grin faded. "Not feeling well?"

"No, no, I'm fine. Just tired. How 'bout I sleep a little longer, then join you all?"

"The boys will be leaving soon. I thought you might want to visit."

Uncoiling her body, Paige pushed herself to a sitting position. With thumb and forefinger she swept the hair back from her brow. Her stomach churned; she swallowed hard against the rising bile. "You're right. I'll just shower and get dressed." Using her mother's shoulder for leverage, she rose, then stumbled into the adjoining bathroom in time to lose what little had remained in her stomach of the evening's fare. She was gasping for breath, bracing herself shakily above the commode when a more steady hand slid around her waist and another smoothed the hair back from her face.

"Better?"

Paige could only nod between increasingly deep breaths. She straightened slowly and covered her mother's hand. "Thanks."

"Don't thank me. I just wish there was something I could do for you."

Leaning over the sink, Paige splashed water on her face and rinsed her mouth, then dried herself with the towel Laura offered.

"You're here, Mom. That's enough."

Laura's expression was unreadable, at least to Paige, who still felt shaky. "Will you be all right now?"

Balancing herself against the sink, Paige nodded and smiled as if to prove it. Her smile must have been lacking, for Laura appeared far from convinced, but when a distant "Grandma!" echoed from the hall, her eyes widened.

"Uh-oh. I'd better catch Melissa before she barges in here. You'll be able to make it into the shower by yourself?"

"Yes, I'll be able to make it into the shower by myself."

"You're sure?"

"Mother..."

"All right, Paige. I'm going." She moved toward the door, shaking her head in renewed dismay. "I'm going."

Alone at last, Paige braced her hands on her hips and hung her head. She'd suspected it wouldn't be easy, but one small part of her had dared hope that her mother would share her excitement. Laura was torn; that much was obvious. Paige had to believe that, in time, she'd come around. Her father might either speed up or retard that process; she could only pray that it would be the former. For, as confident as she was in the course she'd chosen, she desperately wanted, needed, the approval and support of those she loved.

BY EARLY SUNDAY EVENING, Paige was alone with her mother in the house once again. Her father had gone to take the last of her brothers to the airport, leaving a pervasive silence in contrast to the constant noise and motion that had existed such a short time before.

Much as Paige had enjoyed seeing her brothers and their families and had wished they might stay longer, she was exhausted. Within minutes of their departure, she fell asleep on the sofa in the den, rousing only to stumble to bed at her mother's urging, remaining there in the deepest of sleep for the rest of the night.

Morning found her feeling decidedly refreshed. The sun was shining on a magnificent autumn day. Wearing jeans and a sweater, Paige made a slice of dry toast, poured herself a glass of juice and took them out to the deep willow-shaded hollow that had always been her favorite backyard spot. Sliding down against the trunk of a tree, she began to nibble on the toast. Overhead, the breeze whispered through gracefully weeping branches. She looked up at her pale green umbrella, took a deep breath and smiled. The smile froze in place, though, when the sound of footsteps announced the approach of her father. Her eyes collided with his, and she bit her lower lip, let it slowly slide out from between her teeth.

Phillip Mattheson came to a halt several feet from her, his gaze never once leaving her face. He was a handsome man, with his shock of dashing gray hair neatly combed and his skin tanned and weathered from hours on the golf course. The casual slacks and jacket he wore did justice to his still-sturdy build. Only his mouth, set in a straight line, and his dark, somber eyes hinted at his concern.

Paige silently returned his gaze, unaware that her own brimmed with trepidation. But Phillip saw it and softened helplessly. Taking another step forward, he hunkered down by her side.

"How're you feeling?" he asked quietly.

"Okay." She waited cautiously for him to say something. When he didn't, but dropped his gaze to her stomach, then the grass, she knew. "Mother told you, didn't she?" He nodded, eyes still averted, and she went on. "I asked her not to. I wanted to tell you myself."

"When I came home last night I was concerned to find you'd already gone to bed. She was concerned herself. I think she just needed to share her worry." His eyes lifted to the subject of their discussion. Laura was making her way across the yard, carrying two mugs of coffee.

"There's no need to worry," Paige stated as her mother came up and handed one of the mugs to Phillip. Laura did look more relaxed, as though relieved of a great weight. Paige couldn't find it in her heart to be angry. In truth she was envious of a relationship that was so close after all these years.

"Coffee, dear?" Laura extended the second mug. When Paige made a faint grimace in distaste, Laura smiled. "I didn't think so." Lifting the mug to her lips, she spoke against its rim. "I never could drink coffee myself when I was pregnant." She took a sip.

Pregnant. The word echoed loudly. Paige cast a wary glance at her father, only to find him scowling at his coffee. She looked for some diversion, but couldn't bear the thought of either orange juice or toast. Threading her fingers through the grass, she pressed her palm to the ground.

"I'm sorry if I've upset you both," she murmured. "I wish I could have done things the way you might have wanted, but it just didn't work out that way."

"Why didn't it?" her father asked. "From what your mother said, you loved this . . . Jesse."

"I did—do. But one-sided love can't make a marriage."

"He didn't love you?"

Paige pulled at the glass. "I don't know."

Laura settled herself on the ground. "How can you not know something like that? It's either there . . . or it isn't."

"I don't think it's as simple as that," Paige replied, voicing the thoughts she'd spent the past two months sorting out. "Jesse may have loved me on one plane, but on another he couldn't cope with the concept of love." She raised beseechful eyes to meet those of her father. "He's a very special man, very sensitive in his way. But he didn't grow up the way we did. His mother resented his existence. His father was nowhere in sight. He was trained in the school of hard knocks and is convinced that that's the only way he can live." She took a breath, then went on with pride. "He's very talented, a successful film editor."

"Your mother told me. How long was it he stayed in Marblehead?"

"Six weeks." She anticipated her father's response and sought to nip it in the bud. "But he wasn't a free-loader. During the time he was there, I didn't open my wallet once. He paid for food, restaurants, movies. He repaired countless things that needed fixing around the house, again at his own expense."

"That was generous of him," Phillip grunted, slipping from his haunches to the ground, stretching out his legs, crossing them at the ankles. Paige knew he was less relaxed than he looked, but her main concern was in defending Jesse.

"It *was* generous. He didn't have to do those things. I was perfectly willing to have him stay as my guest. He needed a vacation, and I thought my house would be the perfect place. But he made it clear at the beginning that he intended to carry his weight."

Phillip seemed unimpressed. "Carry his weight, huh? Looks to me more like he's foisted it on you."

"The baby was my idea, Daddy." She shot a glance at her mother. "I told you that." When she looked back at her father, his expression was guarded. "I decided on my own that I wanted this child. I knew Jesse would be leaving. I also knew that if I'd have suggested it he'd have packed and left right then. So don't blame him for my being pregnant. If anyone's to blame, it's me. If he found out, he'd probably be as furious as you are."

Reaching out, Phillip squeezed her shoulder in a way that gave Paige her first measure of comfort. "I'm not furious, sweetheart. I'm worried. Do you have any idea what you face? Raising a child in this day and age is hard enough under normal circumstances. You're starting with a distinct disadvantage."

"I've thought that all through, Daddy, and I don't think it'll be so bad. I've got a solid career, an ideal one in fact for a single mother. I work at home, so I can gear my schedule around that of a child. I make good money—"

"Money isn't an issue," her father interrupted with a dismissing wave of his hand. "We'll help you out. You know that."

"I do know that, and it's a comfort, but I don't *need* it. I can easily support my child and myself on what I earn. Besides, you've already done so much. Thanks to you I've got blue-chip stocks, interest in any number of real-estate ventures, plus a healthy trust fund that I can tap in case of emergency. I've got a big, beautiful house whose value only increases. I live in a safe area. My neighbors are all well-to-do and reputable—"

"But you'll be alone." This time it was Laura who interrupted. "The material aspect of child rearing is only one part of it. What about the emotional part? How will you explain to your child that he doesn't have a father?"

Paige answered her with the same quiet deliberation. "There are too many single-parent homes nowadays for that to be a problem. With the divorce rate what it is, there'll be plenty of other children in similar circumstances. As for what I'll tell the child when he's old enough to know, I'll tell him the truth—that I loved his father very much, that his father is a special man who would have loved him deeply if he'd been there."

"Do you honestly believe that?" Phillip asked skeptically. "From what you've said, the man didn't want any part of a child."

Paige lowered her eyes. "That was what he said, but I've seen him with children and he's wonderful. I think it's the responsibility he fears, the emotional responsibility. He sees the world as a pretty awful place and he doesn't want to bring a child into it. Maybe he's trying to spare himself some kind of pain."

"How can you be so . . . so forgiving?" Laura gasped.

"Not forgiving, Mom. There's nothing to forgive. Jesse laid his feelings on the line when we first got together. He was forthright from the start. I'm the one who was slightly devious in letting him believe I was using birth control. No, forgiving isn't the word. Accepting, perhaps. But then, you both taught me that. I can only do my best. That's what you've always said. I can't beat my head against a brick wall if my best isn't perfect. I have to reconcile myself, to accept the facts as they are and be proud of what I did do."

Her voice softened, taking on a pleading note. "That's what I want from you now. Acceptance. The facts are—" she raised one finger "—that I'm pregnant and—" she raised a second "—that I'm very, very happy about it. I want you to be pleased, too." She looked from Phillip to Laura and back. "I want to know that you'll be there to share my excitement when the baby's born, that my child will have grandparents who love him as much as I do." Her hand fell to her stomach in an instinctively possessive grip. "Because I do love this child and I'm going to have it and raise it, and nothing, nothing in the world can change those facts."

Before she could do so much as take a breath, her father had reached out and drawn her into his arms. "We wouldn't want to change them, sweetheart," he crooned huskily, his arms strong about her back. "We're proud of you. Always have been, always will be."

Paige felt her eyes fill with tears and pressed her face into his welcoming shoulder. "Thanks, Daddy," she whispered. "I needed that." When she finally raised her head, it was to seek out her mother. One half wasn't enough; she needed them both.

Laura's eyes were as moist as Paige's, but her lips curved into a tentative smile. "I couldn't agree with your father more, darling." She tipped up her chin. "And if the ladies of my bridge club are shocked, I'll tell them to . . . to . . ." As defiant as she suddenly felt, the coarse words on the tip of her tongue couldn't quite make it past her lips. She blushed, then laughed and leaned forward to hug Paige herself. When at last she held her back, it was to look lovingly at her face.

"You've always been a determined one, Paige. I'm proud of that, too. You will, I'm sure, make a wonderful mother." To counter the weepiness she felt, she feigned sudden sternness. "*If* you ever make it. You've got to take care of yourself, dear. Better still—" her eyes lit up "—*I'll* take care of you. Why don't I drive back up with you? I'll only stay a week or so. I can cook and clean and hold your head when you throw up—"

"Mother!" Paige laughed, feeling incredibly light-hearted. "I do believe that's above and beyond the call of duty."

But Laura simply straightened her shoulders. "I did it yesterday and I'll do it again. Nothing is above and beyond the call of duty when it comes to those you love."

IN THE DAYS THAT FOLLOWED, Laura was as good as her word. Though she allowed Paige to sculpt, she permitted her nothing else by way of work. For a woman who had always had a housekeeper, Laura took surprising joy in seeing to all the needs of Paige's home. She cleaned with a vengeance and cooked up a storm, stocking the freezer with so much food that Paige wouldn't have to do much more than operate the microwave oven for the next few months.

Though Paige wasn't used to such pampering, she found that the rest did her good. Whether the improvement had to do with her mother's care or with the fact that the critical first three months of pregnancy were now behind her, she didn't know. But by the time Laura left, Paige was feeling far better than she had in weeks. It was a good thing. For, once more, she was alone.

8

IN THE WEEKS that followed, Paige continued to grow physically and emotionally stronger. That she missed Jesse was a given, but she'd come to terms with his absence and was redirecting her energy toward preparation for the birth of their child.

Their child. She did think of it that way. It thrilled her to know that it was Jesse's child in her belly, that she'd always have that little part of him. Oh, yes, she knew that psychologists would say she was loving her child in place of her man, but they were wrong. There was nothing "in place of" about the love she felt for the unborn babe. It was more a matter of "in addition to." The child would have its own love and then some.

By the end of her fourth month, she was filled with energy and sculpting furiously, intent on supplying the galleries with enough work to keep the owners satisfied during that time around the baby's birth when she'd be unable to sculpt. She'd finally told Marjory about her pregnancy, and smiled every time she recalled that conversation.

"You're *what*?"

"I'm pregnant."

"You've got to be kidding."

"Nope."

"*Pregnant*? I don't believe it."

Paige had grinned. "It's true."

"What is this, the second coming? Come on, love. Immaculate conception isn't for mortals."

"It wasn't immaculate conception."

"Then you've been holding out on me. Who is he?"

For reasons she hadn't understood at the time, Paige had never mentioned Jesse's presence when Marjory had called. Now she realized that there had been a part of her that had wanted it to be her secret, another part that had half feared Marjory's inevitable teasing.

Now there was a completely different reason why she wouldn't tell Marjory about Jesse. Though she trusted her, she didn't want to burden her with secrecy. It was a small world. Too easily word could spread. The last thing Paige wanted was for Jesse to learn through the grapevine that he'd fathered a child.

"Who he is is irrelevant," Paige had answered gently. "He was here for a time and I loved him, but now he's gone. I wanted the baby. He doesn't know anything about it."

There had been a long, uncharacteristic silence from Marjory. When she'd finally spoken, it had been on the recovery side of stupefaction. "You are truly remarkable, Paige Mattheson. Cool, dispassionate Paige Mattheson. Ice maiden?" She'd nearly choked in delight. "I still don't believe it!" But she was excited, and Paige was pleased. "If ever I'd expect to hear something astounding from you, it wouldn't have been this! A baby... my God! That's fantastic! You *are* full of surprises!" She'd chuckled. "For your sake, I hope the stars don't converge on the night it's born. No one will ever believe you then!"

Paige had laughed with her, but the conversation had held far deeper import. Indeed, the fact of her pregnancy made lie of the ice-maiden image. There would be those who'd be shocked. But Paige was proud, proud to be pregnant, proud to have done something she wanted to do. Through Marjory's eyes she'd glimpsed a new image of herself. The cool, self-possessed sculptress of stone was going to be a mother.

JESSE DALLAS, of course, knew nothing of this. He only knew, as he held his foot to the gas pedal, that he had to see Paige. For four months he'd worked himself to the limit, praying that one day he'd awaken without her image before his eyes.

It hadn't happened. When he'd pushed himself all the harder, he'd managed only to view that image through a migraine headache. The migraine passed; the image did not. More than once, in desperation, he'd called a number from his little black book. The consequences had been embarrassing. He'd finally given up on that particular potential diversion, fearing for his reputation, if not his sanity.

Exorcism was what was needed, he'd decided. He'd drive up and see Paige, be his arrogant self, provoke what was certain to be anger on her part—after all, he hadn't so much as dropped her a postcard in the months he'd been gone—and then return to New York. He'd be done with her. Free. Oh, Lord, what he'd give for freedom once more!

Leaving the highway, he turned onto the local roads he remembered so well. The trees were bare now, as dictated by the November chill. Though the snows hadn't yet come, there was promise in the air. He'd go skiing, perhaps in the Alps; would even dare, with Paige's image banished once and for all, to pick up a warm and cuddly snowbunny for his evening's delight.

Thoughts of snowbunnies left his mind the instant he turned onto the road that wound along the shore. There was a barren beauty about winter's ocean with its slate-gray hue and prancing whitecaps. The roar of the waves overpowered the hungry purr of his car, and he felt suddenly threatened. He liked this place. Even in winter it beckoned. He wished it had been a rainy day, cold and raw and forbidding. But it wasn't. And he was here. Pulling into Paige's driveway, he stopped the car.

The house looked just the same, blending into the late November winterscape as snugly as it had stood out refreshingly in the summer's heat. Trying to ignore the excitement that flashed through his veins, he tucked his keys in his jacket pocket, pulled up his collar and started up the walk. Thrusting his hands in his pockets for warmth, he approached the door. On impulse, he dragged his keys back out, fingering them, singling out the one that fit Paige's lock. He'd never given it back. Had she had the locks changed?

She hadn't. The key slid in smoothly. He turned it, slowly pushed the door open and looked inside. At once the serenity of the place enveloped him. Even as he tried to deny its grip he was drawn in. Closing the door as soundlessly as he'd opened it, he turned around. The same. It was exactly the same.

Paige was nowhere in sight. He started down the hall toward the bedroom, then turned and headed for the other wing, realizing that she'd more likely be in the studio. He'd surprise her. Perhaps scare the wits out of her. She *should* have had the lock changed. Men were an irresponsible lot.

As always the studio door was open. Jesse found himself slowing as he approached, walking stealthily, with a trace of hesitation. It was almost as if he neared that same invisible barrier he'd encountered when he'd first come here. And as he had then, he now sensed he was intruding. It was callous of him to come back this way, but he'd had to. There'd been no choice.

Taking the last steps with quiet determination, he came to a halt on the threshold and helplessly caught his breath. She was there, head bowed over a piece of stone in her lap. He saw nothing but her. Wearing an oversize sweatshirt that bore streaks of dust, a pair of jeans that hugged her thighs and calves, she was deep in concentration, easing an abrasive strip back and forth over the stone. She wore no mask this time, so her hair fell freely, creating a shimmering shield that hid her features from him.

He took one step into the room, then another. His eyes never left her bent head. Farther he came, slowly, making barely a sound. Barely. But the tile underfoot wasn't as forgiving as the outer carpeting had been. He'd crossed no more than half the distance between them when the heel of his shoe scraped the floor.

Paige's head flew up, her eyes wide in alarm. Her lips parted as if she'd cry out, but no sound came. She stared, blinked, stared again. All color drained from her cheeks. She lowered her head, pressed her eyes shut, rubbed the bridge of her nose. Then she looked up again, this time not so much in fear as in disbelief.

"Jesse?" she whispered.

He could do nothing but nod. His vocal cords seemed stuck.

"You're . . . here?" Still that incredulous whisper.

Again he nodded.

Her eyes went even wider, and she swallowed once. Then, in a concise burst of movement, she was off the stool and into his arms. The stone she'd been smoothing fell unnoticed to the floor, as did the sandbags on which it had rested and the large burlap mat.

Jesse hadn't been aware that he'd held out his arms until they'd caught her, closed about her slender form and lifted her clear off her feet. For the first time in months and months he felt happy. He closed his eyes, pressed his face to her hair and held her so tightly that his hands crisscrossed her back to grasp opposite sides of her waist. He couldn't believe how wonderful she felt, so warm and soft and tremblingly alive. He couldn't even object to her choke-hold on his neck. It made him feel . . . needed.

"Jesse?" she whispered once more, releasing his neck and pushing herself back so that she could see his face. With great reluctance he loosened his arms, but he didn't let her go.

"It's me." He gave her a crooked smile. "In the flesh."

His attempt at humor sailed over her head. "I can't believe it! Oh, Jesse!" Her arms were about his neck again, squeezing tightly, her breath trembling by his ear. "I can't believe it! I thought I'd never see you again!"

"Now, did I ever say that?"

It was as though she never heard his drawl. "God, it's good to see you!" She pushed back again. "Let me look."

He was enjoying every bit of her excitement. "I thought that was what you did a second ago."

Unfazed, she let her eyes drop his full length. "You look so big," she whispered in near-awe.

"It's the jacket." Suede, with a thick sheepskin lining, the jacket may have indeed magnified his size. But he was a large man even without it.

Exquisitely appreciative, Paige took in the breadth of his shoulders, then looked up at his face again. She brushed back the swathe of sandy hair that had fallen across his brow and frowned. "You look tired. You've been working too hard."

His lips twitched. "You could say that."

"Is the film done?"

"That one, and a second." He paused, watching closely for her reaction. She had to realize that he'd taken at least a few days off between the two. "I'm a louse. I never called or wrote. It's been four months and now I have the nerve to show up on your doorstep. Come on. Tell me what a bastard I am."

To his astonishment, she simply grinned. "In time. God, you look great, baggy eyes and all!" She hugged him again and, for an instant, Jesse thought he'd like to stay forever like that, with her clinging to him as though he really, really mattered. He knew it was an illusion, and wondered why he was suddenly prone to such fancy, but other thoughts were beginning to intrude— like how firm and full her breasts felt against him, how shapely her hips were beneath his now-wandering hands, how perfectly her entire body fit against his. He pushed illusion aside to concentrate on a very real primal drive.

"I need you, Paige," he growled against her ear. "You may not believe this, but I haven't been able to make it with another woman since I left."

"That's quite a confession."

"It's the truth. I tried. Believe me, I tried. But it wasn't any good. You've ruined me."

"I must have. Something's definitely wrong. You haven't even kissed me yet."

He was the one to draw back then, the expression on his face comical in its astonishment. "I haven't?"

"Not . . . once."

His gaze dropped to her lips, studying them almost hypnotically. Fingers trembling, he slid his hands up to frame her face, caressing her even as they held her still. Then he took a shuddering breath that emerged in a moan and crushed his lips to hers.

His fierceness was just what Paige needed. She didn't care that he'd called other women before he'd come back to her. The only thing that mattered was that he had, indeed, come back.

The kiss she returned was no more gentle than the one he gave. After months of craving, their hunger was mutual and explosive. Greedy lips slanted and grasped. Avid tongues fought for the honeyed moisture beyond. Heated breath mingled, producing urgent moans. And all the while impatient hands clutched shoulders, backs, hips in avaricious reacquaintance.

"Oh, God," Jesse panted, "God, I need you."

"I need you, too," Paige whispered, clinging so tightly to his neck that her arms shook.

"Come on." Unwinding her arms from his neck, he took her hand and began striding across the tile floor. She had to run to keep up as he led her quickly toward the other wing and her bedroom. When he released her to tug off his coat, she dashed into the bathroom, emerging a minute later to find that he'd pulled back the covers and was bare from the waist up.

She thrust her jeans down her legs while he dispensed with his own. Her sweatshirt was just clearing her head when his hands found her breasts. Her entire body quivered with such rampant desire that she thought she'd burst.

"Hurry," she gasped, peeling down her panties, kicking them aside, then reaching for the waistband of his briefs. He released her breasts to assist her. Within seconds they were tumbling back on the bed in each other's arms. Her whisper was hoarse and intense. "I need you! God, Jesse, I need you . . . inside . . . !"

He was there then, filling the void that had gnawed at her so long. The groan that came from her throat told of a precious, sweet pain, one he echoed in kind.

They took each other in a frenzy, demanding without mercy or shame. It was as though neither could get enough, as though the physical limitations of their bodies frustrated the emotional bond between them. If Paige was driven wild by the love she felt, Jesse was no less frantic in his need to absorb her whole. Their bodies slammed slickly against each other, hips thrusting in their bid for oneness.

When it came, it was simultaneous and heart-stopping. Paige's breath caught in her throat; Jesse gave a hoarse cry. Their arched bodies were suspended, then shattered in endless spasms that left them quivering.

It was a long time before either spoke, before either could catch his breath to produce so much as a whimper. Paige felt she'd been to heaven and back. She'd never in her life felt so . . . blessed.

"Ahhhhh," Jesse murmured at last. He pressed his lips to her forehead, left them there while he inhaled shakily, then slid an arm beneath her and brought her curving to his side. "I've missed you, love. Damn it, I've missed you."

She understood his reluctance and it only added to her satisfaction. The fact that he'd come back to her *against* his will said something for the depth of his feeling. True, perhaps the feeling was primarily physical. But it was something.

"I've missed you too, Jesse."

He took one deep breath, and another, then moaned and turned his body toward hers. "You're a witch, I think. You've got me under a wicked spell."

"No spell." She slid her hand across his chest, loving its damp warmth, loving the way the dark golden hair tickled her palm. "I can't believe it," she whispered, astonished once again. She raised her head to give him an owl-eyed stare. "I keep thinking I've imagined you."

He chuckled. "If you think that was a ghost inside you just now, you've really gone off the deep end."

"No ghost?"

"No ghost."

Smiling, she settled her head back in the crook of his shoulder, rubbing her cheek against the softer flesh beside his armpit. "I'm glad you're here."

"So am I." His eyes trailed down her body then, appreciating it at a more leisurely pace. His free hand soon followed, heating her tired flesh anew. "Your breasts are so full." He traced a faint blue vein, amazed he'd never noticed it before, but before he could ask he was distracted by the responsive erection of her nipple. Dipping his head, he kissed the taut nub. "Mmm. It always was good with us," he murmured. "It still is. I take one look at you and, bam, I'm up. And you're always ready."

His words, uttered in such a husky timbre, were as stirring to Paige as his nearness. She arched against his hip, sliding her leg between his. Her own smoothness against his more textured flesh never failed to excite her. She drew the sole of her foot along his calf to his knee, then reversed direction.

The movement drew Jesse's eyes downward. He slid his hand to her hip, then her belly. His palm caressed it, gliding over and around the faintly curved surface. Strange, his hand remembered a perfectly flat ivory plane. This tiny bulge was new. He frowned for an instant, wondering if she'd gained weight. If she'd been pining over him, surely the opposite would have been the case, particularly since she'd never been a hearty eater.

Skimming her body, he saw that her limbs were as slim and shapely as ever. It was only her belly . . . and her breasts. . . .

An awful thought jolted him. But . . . *that* wouldn't have happened. It *couldn't* have. There had been that one episode when she might have been vulnerable, but she'd gotten her period after that. And henceforth she'd been protected. Hadn't she run into the bathroom even today?

His gaze flew to her face. Her eyes were closed, her lips curved in a half kiss against him. When he touched her cheek, she smiled and purred. He trailed his fingers over her throat to her breast, circling its vein-shadowed fullness until she squirmed against him.

He opened his mouth to ask her point-blank, then closed it. If he'd been imagining something that wasn't true, he'd feel like a fool. But . . . there was one way he could tell. One sure way.

His touch grew more caressive on her breasts, and he eased himself lower until his mouth found hers. His kiss was deliberately seductive, teasing and coaxing while his hand slid lower. She moaned and opened to him, kissing him back, happily stroking his arms and the rippling musculature of his back.

He rubbed her belly, very, very gently, before inching even lower. His fingers were silky, insinuating themselves into her warmth as they'd done so often in the past, evoking the same soft gasps of delight. Deeper they crept, tantalizing her most sensitive spots, finally sliding farther, searching . . .

Then they were gone.

Dazed and in ecstasy, Paige didn't feel the stiffening of Jesse's limbs. The loss of his touch, though, left her bereft. Opening her eyes to urge him back, she met a scowling countenance that was instant ice to her ardor.

"Jesse?" she asked in alarm, eyes widening. "What is it?"

"Your diaphragm. It's not there."

She swallowed once. "I know."

"Where is it?"

Her heart was pounding but she kept her voice calm. "In its case in the medicine chest."

"Why isn't it in you?"

"I . . . I don't need it."

As she watched, he flicked his gaze to her breasts, then her stomach. "And that little dash into the bathroom a few minutes ago?"

She took a tremulous breath. "I had to go." Her voice dropped to a whisper as she confirmed what she knew he'd already guessed. "It's that way with me now."

His jaw flexed once then froze. His blue eyes hardened. His nostrils flared. Then he was pushing himself up on a fist and tipping his head back. "Goddammit!" he bellowed. When he looked back at her, his rage was barely contained. "How did it happen? *How in the hell did it happen?*"

"You know the facts of life," she said quietly.

"Yeah, but that thing was supposed to protect you. Do you mean to say that we're in the small percentage for whom it doesn't work?"

"No. That's not the case."

"Then what is, damn it, *what is*?"

She made no attempt to dodge his gaze. "I didn't use my diaphragm that last night, Jesse. It's as simple as that."

"As simple...you didn't use..." He loomed over her, pinning her shoulders to the sheets. She cringed, but only because she truly believed he was angry enough to hit her. "What in the hell possessed you to do *that*?" he roared, fingers digging into her flesh.

Her lower lip trembled, but her tone remained firm. "I decided I wanted a baby. I knew you were leaving. I believed at the time that I'd never see you again."

"You decided. *You* decided? And I was just the dumb stud in the deal?"

"It wasn't like that. It was *your* baby I wanted."

He released her shoulders abruptly. "Great. You decided you wanted to have *my* baby, so you took things into your own hands. Didn't you have the guts to discuss it with me?"

Feeling as naked in the face of his hostility as she truly was, she struggled up and reached for the sheet. "I knew what your feelings were. You'd made them very clear—"

"Oh-ho, no," he growled, snatching the sheet from her fingers. "You won't hide from me. If you've got my baby in your belly, I've got a right to see everything!"

In a flare of anger, she faced him. "Right? *Right?* You have no right! You were the one who took off without a second glance, who let four months, *four months* pass without a word." She flung out her hand. "You saw other women, you did God knows what during that time, and never once did you so much as give me a call to see if I was okay." She took a sharp breath. "Don't talk to me of rights, Jesse Dallas! You haven't got *any* in my life!"

In the wake of her outburst, he seemed to gain a measure of control. "That may have been true at one time, Paige," he stated, "but you're carrying my child now. That changes things a bit."

"And just how does it change them? You're free to leave now, to go back to that hard life you feed off. How in the devil does my pregnancy change anything?"

"It's my child—"

She jabbed at her chest. "It's my child, too. And since I'm the only one who wants it, I take sole responsibility."

"I'll bet you do," he snarled.

"And just what is that supposed to mean?"

"It means that I can imagine what little plots you've got in that devious mind of yours. When were you going to tell me, Paige? When it was too late for an abortion?" He took perverse pleasure when she flinched. "When you were on the verge of giving birth and needed someone to hold your hand? Or was I going to get a little court order out of the blue demanding child support?"

Her hand clenched into a fist over her stomach. She tried to still the quaking of her limbs but they refused to obey her silent command. Mustering her pride, she inched up her chin. "I wasn't going to tell you at all. The way I saw it, it was my business, and my business alone. I'd decided I wanted to conceive and I did. I didn't consult you. It wasn't your choice." She kept talking as Jesse stormed up and stalked around the bed to stand at her side, glaring down. "I knew precisely what I was doing *and* what the consequences would be."

"You don't know anything about consequences! You grew up insulated in a suburban cocoon. You haven't the faintest—"

"Don't start in on that!" she interrupted, surging to her knees in frustration. "I'm tired of hearing about the mean world out there. Your view is *warped*. Has anyone ever told you that?"

"Screw that world!" He thrust a pointed finger toward the floor. "I'm talking about the responsibility of day-to-day child rearing. How're you going to sculpt with a squalling kid around? And if you can't sculpt, how are you going to be able to feed it? And even *if* you get beyond the squalling and feeding, how in the hell are you going to be able to give the child what it needs? You're a woman. Just a woman. A kid needs a father, too."

"I may be *just* a woman, but I've got enough love to more than cover what's lacking from a stone-cold father. I've got plenty of money whether I work for the next five years or not, and I refuse to believe that I won't be able to work. Face it, Jesse. Single mothers have been doing it for years now."

"Yeah, I know how well they do it. You forget I grew up in a home like that."

"I'm going to ignore that comment," she stated, deadly quiet.

He made a face and gestured broadly. "I didn't mean that you'd whore. I know you wouldn't do that."

"Well, thank you."

Her sarcasm was ignored as Jesse ranted on. "I'm talking about resentment. When you're in the middle of a tricky piece of work and the baby starts to bawl, you're going to resent it. And it'll only get worse. You take off to go to New York for a show, and you've got this albatross hanging around your neck. You want to date—okay, even an innocent date—and the baby-sitter calls to cancel at the last minute. It'll be hell."

Paige squared her shoulders. "Maybe it was for your mother, but it won't be for me. Because I want this child and I love it already. Don't you see? When it comes to this baby, I don't *care* about my work. I don't care about New York. I don't care about dating. And besides, even if I did need to get away, my parents would be up here to stay with the baby before I could blink an eyelash."

Jesse straightened, hands falling from their imperious perch on his hips. He seemed suddenly unsure. "Your parents? You've told your parents you're pregnant?"

"Of course." She frowned. "Did you think I wouldn't?"

"Were they... angry?"

"Angry? No. Stunned perhaps, at first, and worried, then excited. You see, Jesse, they love me. My happiness is theirs." She sighed. "I wish you could have met them. As parents go, they're so different from anything you've known. They care, truly care about every aspect of my life. They've given me the strength to face things, which is one of the reasons the prospect of single-motherhood doesn't scare me. Furthermore, I know that I can give my child that same kind of strength, so that it will be able to face whatever comes along."

Jesse stared at her. "You're crazy. *All* of you."

"We could say the same about you," she said softly. "You can't begin to imagine the joy of holding a baby in your arms, having its tiny finger curl around yours, having it cling to your neck as if it can't live without you. You can't imagine the pride you feel when it gets its first tooth, when it takes its first steps, when it says 'Mama' for the first time—"

"'It'…'it'…must you make it sound like you've got some kind of neuter being in there?"

There was a petulance in his tone that made Paige smile. "What would you have me say? If I say 'he,' I'd be called sexist. If I say 'she,' I could well be wrong."

Having no answer to that, Jesse's brows lowered. "And how do you know about the joys, anyway? You've never been a mother and *you* were the baby of your family."

"I didn't say *know*. I said *imagine*. But I do have nieces and nephews and I remember when they were small."

"Somebody else's kid is one thing. You can give it back when it gets to be a pain."

"I won't want to give this one back. I *want* it. I want to be a mother."

Jesse muttered something unintelligible as he turned to retrieve his jeans. "You know, Paige, I never would have expected this of you." His voice jolted with the movement as he angrily pulled the denim over his legs. He tugged up his zipper and straightened. "It's really pretty funny. Remember that day you insisted on going to the doctor? You said you couldn't trust *me*."

She hadn't thought about that day. Now she felt a brief pang of guilt. "I was only kidding."

"Well, it sure as hell worked to your benefit, didn't it?"

"I hadn't planned a thing at the time. You have to believe that, Jesse."

He scooped his shirt from the floor. "When *did* you start planning this little fiasco?" He glared. "A week later? Or two? Or did it come to you when you got your period and realized it hadn't taken that first time?"

She spoke slowly and with deliberation. "I didn't plan a thing until that very last night. It just . . . came to me when I was in the bathroom."

"Just came to you," he ridiculed. "Like the secret of the stone?"

"No! I—"

"If what you're saying is true," he interrupted, "you couldn't have had much of a chance to think *anything* out!"

"I knew it was right. Call it intuition or whatever, but every sense I possessed told me it was right."

Shirt hanging open, he raked his hand through his hair. "Intuition. Oh, please." The scorn in his voice was mirrored by the disgust on his face. But before Paige could speak to defend herself, he'd turned on his heel and charged out of the room.

She sat in stunned paralysis for what seemed an eternity before reaching for the covers and drawing them up. Then, curling up on the mattress, she struggled to calm herself as reaction set in. She trembled uncontrollably and felt chilled to the bone. Tugging the covers more closely around her neck didn't help. Neither did an attempt to focus her thoughts on the baby whose existence meant so very much to her.

She hurt.

Recollection of how happy she'd been to see Jesse, of how ecstatic their coming together had been on this very same bed, served only to sharpen the pain within. The contrast was stark—from rapture to hell. She wished he'd never come back, if only to have been spared his anger. Surely he'd leave again, this time truly for good. She much preferred to remember him the way he'd been the last time—loving, if she dared say so— than to remember him as the hard, unfeeling man he'd been in his fury just now.

Closing her eyes against the misery she felt, she tried to place what had happened into the overall scheme of things. This was a setback, that was all. She'd go ahead with her plans and do the best she could in pushing Jesse from her mind. A setback, just a setback. Somehow she sensed, though, that she'd be a long time in recovering.

It all boiled down to one thing. Her dream was shattered. Before, when Jesse knew nothing of the baby and she pictured him going about his life in New York, she'd been able to imagine from time to time that, had he known about the child, he might have been pleased. Oh, yes, it was an illusion, but a harmless one. Now, illusion was delusion, thoroughly harmful, totally unacceptable. The sooner Jesse left, the better.

She lay still, listening, wondering where he was. His coat was still on the chair, so he had to be in the house, unless he'd rushed out into the cold with just his anger to keep him warm. She'd heard no door banging, but she hadn't heard him come in, either. Then she'd been engrossed in her work, a plausible enough excuse. Perhaps now she'd been deafened by misery. Spotting one dark loafer across the room, she realized that he couldn't have gone far. Oh, yes, he'd be back, and she sensed there'd be more unpleasantness before he finally left.

With a weary sigh, she pushed herself up. If she had to field his disdain once more, she'd need all the help she could get. Her clothes would be a start; at least then she wouldn't feel so vulnerable.

Sitting on the edge of the bed, she gingerly pulled her sweatshirt on over her head. Her muscles felt stiff and tense and tired, but she knew they simply reflected the ache radiating from her heart. Lifting one leg, then the other, she tugged on her jeans. She stood only for the second it took to ease them up over her hips, then sank weakly back on the bed. Propping herself on shaky arms, she closed her eyes and willed strength to her spent limbs.

That was how Jesse found her when he stalked back into the room. He came to an abrupt halt, taking in her weary pose, her closed eyes, the milky pallor of her skin. She was slower to react, his footsteps having been muted by the rug, but a sixth sense warned her he'd returned, and she opened her eyes and stiffened.

"Are you all right?" he asked evenly.

"Yes." Lowering her gaze, she closed the zipper of her jeans, but when it came to the snap, which was sorely tried at best, her seated position and boneless fingers conspired against her.

Jesse watched her fumblings with a frown. "Leave it undone. You'll only suffocate the kid."

"I will not—"

He cut off her denial. "If you can't even look out for the baby's best interests now, I can just imagine what it'll be like later on."

Paige was incensed. "I've managed just fine up until now, and I'll manage just fine in the future."

"Hmph." He looked around for his socks, then his shoes. "Get something on your feet. We've got things to do."

"What things?" she asked warily.

He sat in the chair and pushed his foot into a sock. "Blood tests. A license."

Paige felt the blood drain from her face. "License?" she whispered.

"That's right. We're getting married."

"What?"

He had the other sock on and was pushing his feet into his shoes. "You heard me." Standing, he eyed her critically. "If you want to change your clothes, fine. You should be wearing looser things, anyway. If you haven't bought any maternity clothes, we'll stop for those, too."

"Wait...just...one...minute." She shook her head, trying to ingest what he'd said. "Back up a little. We're getting *married*?"

"Yes." He was on his feet, clearly annoyed. "Damn it, Paige, you're wasting time—"

"Who's getting married?"

"You and me. Now, get a move—"

"I'm not marrying you!" she cried, bolting to her feet only to sway when myriad bright lights exploded before her eyes. Groping for the bed, she sagged back down, gasping for breath, feeling positively ill. Within

seconds her head was being pushed between her knees and a firm hand was rubbing her neck.

"Keep your head down. It'll pass."

"Dizzy..."

"I know. You moved too fast."

She wanted to say that he'd been the one to tell her to move, that he'd been the one to upset her from the start, but she felt too weak to utter a word. With her head down, the blood slowly returned and she revived.

"You're hurting my neck," she murmured.

He raised her shoulders and pushed her hair back from her face. "You're in a cold sweat. Lie down." He was off the bed then and, without his support, she had no choice but to follow his command. When he returned he carried a cool, damp cloth. Sitting beside her on the bed, he pressed it to her forehead.

She put her hand over it and closed her eyes. "I'm not marrying you, Jesse."

"You're carrying my child. You'll marry me."

"You can't force me to."

"You're right. But if you refuse, I'll have to take stronger measures. Once the child's born, I'll go to court for visitation rights. In fact, I may even sue for joint custody. It's the up-and-coming thing. You know, half the year with the mother, half with the father."

Paige's eyes were open now, wide with fear. "You wouldn't," she whispered.

"I most certainly would."

"But... but you don't want the child!"

"Keep your voice down or you'll really make yourself sick."

"Jesse, you can't be serious about all this."

"Why not?"

"You don't want any ties. You don't want a wife. You don't want children."

"I've changed my mind."

"Just like *that*? In ten minutes' time?"

"Seems to me you did much the same, though I don't recall you were in the bathroom that night for more than five."

Closing her eyes again, she turned her face away. "I can't believe this is happening."

"It'll sink in pretty quick. You'll be my wife by the weekend."

Her head flew back. "No!" At his warning glance, she lowered her voice. "No. You can't marry me, Jesse. You don't love me!"

"Love? What's *love* got to do with anything?"

"It's the basis of most marriages."

"Gimme a break. Most marriages are based on expediency. A man wants a woman to see to his needs, a woman wants a man to give her security. In some cases there may be financial considerations, but most often it's the image of marriage that people fall for. When the image tarnishes, divorce comes into play."

"You are a cynic."

"I think you've said that before."

"Well, it's true. And I suppose the point of expediency in our case is the baby?"

"Good thinking. Your head must be clearing."

Distraught, she rolled onto her side away from him, flinging away the now-tepid cloth as she went. Tucking up her knees, she pressed a protective arm across her middle. "Exactly what do you hope to accomplish, Jesse?"

"By marrying you? I'd have thought it would be obvious." With a sigh, he stood up and walked to the window. It was not quite four, but the sky was darkening already. "Given a choice, I would never have let you conceive. But since the deed's done, I want my kid to have everything I didn't. That means a warm home, plenty of clothes and toys and playmates, the most nourishing of food . . . and above all, two parents."

Paige turned her head and stared at his back. "*Love*, Jesse. That's what you were missing. If you'd had that, none of the other things would have mattered. You're sadly mistaken if you think that I was happy as a child because of the toys or clothes or food I had. It was my parents' love that made my life." She paused. "So if you don't believe in love, what can you possibly offer our child?"

Without turning, Jesse shrugged. His voice was suddenly more distant, less cool, almost . . . soft. "I can be there when he's sick, hold him when he's had a nightmare. I can go to his school plays, take him for fries at McDonald's. I can read to him at night and teach him to play chess. I can swing him up on my shoulders and make him laugh."

For the first time since her own nightmare had begun that afternoon, Paige felt heartened. Though he couldn't realize it, Jesse had just given her a glimpse of the man she loved. Not only that, though he'd be appalled if she suggested it, what he'd described just now sounded suspiciously like a demonstration of love. She felt suddenly lighter, as though a great weight was lifting from her heart.

Then Jesse turned and half the weight settled back. His expression was closed once more. If he'd allowed a bit of warmth to seep through when thinking of his child, he obviously had no intention of extending that warmth to her.

"Are you ready to go?" he asked in a tone compatible with his expression.

She pushed herself to a seated position but made no move to rise from the bed. "Jesse, I think you ought to think this out. You may have decided that you want our child, but you certainly don't want me."

"I wouldn't say that," he drawled with unmistakable intent, but a chill remained in his eyes and she was filled with dread.

"Oh, no, Jesse . . ." she breathed in disbelief.

"Oh, yes, Paige." He began to walk forward. "What greater expedient can a man have than a beautiful woman at his beck and call? It's been damned frustrating these past months. I think you'll meet my needs quite well."

She eyed him defiantly. "I won't marry you. I'll take my chances with the courts."

He continued forward until he reached the bed. "You'll marry me. And you'll marry me soon." He pressed both fists to the sheets and put his face close to hers. Every one of his features was hard. Only with great restraint did she hold still, though her eyes grew wider as he spoke. "That kid is going to have two parents." He enunciated slowly, as though to a dimwit. "And they're going to be husband and wife. Jesse Dallas. Paige Dallas." His eyes flashed with the same iron determination that his clenched jaw conveyed. "If I've got to be responsible for bringing a kid into the world, he's not going to be a bastard like his old man was!"

Finding Paige utterly speechless, he slowly straightened. "Now." He buttoned the cuffs at his wrists. "Are you ready to go?"

"Go?" she whispered hoarsely, then cleared her throat. She was stunned. He'd never said anything about being illegitimate before! Or had he? How many times had he called himself a bastard? Of course, she'd taken it as its less literal meaning. "Uh . . . I . . ."

Her arm was grasped and she was helped to her feet. "We'll go to your doctor for the blood tests. That way I can have a good talk with him. When is your next scheduled appointment?"

She frowned and looked down, struggling to think clearly. "I, uh, I saw her last week. I only go once a month."

"Then it's just as well I can meet her now. I don't want to have to wait another three weeks to have my questions answered."

"Jesse, this is really—"

"Shoes, Paige?" He arched his brows, then went to retrieve her sneakers. After staring at them for a minute, he headed for the closet. "These won't keep anything warm out in that cold." He exchanged the sneakers for a pair of low-heeled leather boots, stopped at her dresser for a pair of high wool socks, then set what he'd gathered into her hands. "Put them on. It's getting late. Things will be closing pretty soon for the day. We've got a hell of a lot to do before that hap-

pens." His warning stare was designed to keep her protest in check, but he needn't have worried. She was far
too overwhelmed by conflicting emotions to utter a
sound.

Numb, she pulled on the socks, then the boots. Indeed they'd counter the winter chill. But the chill in her
heart? She knew the remedy for that would be far more
difficult to find.

9

THE WEDDING TOOK PLACE the following Saturday afternoon and was witnessed only by Paige's parents, who'd come in the night before and who insisted on treating the newlyweds to a celebration dinner immediately after the brief civil ceremony. Independent as he was, Jesse's instinct had been to pick up the tab himself. Anticipating this, Paige had been firm. She'd yielded to practically every other demand he'd made—she'd sat by while Jesse had grilled her doctor as though she was unable to take care of herself, she'd dutifully selected the full maternity wardrobe he'd insisted upon, she'd been shunted to bed each night well before she'd been tired—but where her parents were concerned she put her foot down.

"My father will want to take us out afterward, Jesse. Please, don't give him a fight. I'm his only daughter. If he had his way, he'd be walking me down the aisle in a formal ceremony with all of his friends in attendance. Since that's out of the question, give in at least on a dinner."

"Is that what you'd have wanted—to wear a white gown with a long train and go down on his arm with crowds watching?" Jesse had asked coolly.

"Under these circumstances—no. It'll be hard enough keeping up a front for my parents' sake alone."

That, indeed, was her greatest fear. And she tried, she did try, to smile and act pleased. Her mother, as always, saw through the ruse. They'd returned to the house late Saturday afternoon and Paige was sitting on a chair in the guest bedroom while Laura finished packing. Determined to give Paige and Jesse privacy on their wedding night, the Matthesons were driving back to Connecticut that evening.

With her suitcase finally closed, Laura sat on the edge of the bed facing Paige. "I want you to be happy, darling. Are you sure this is what you want?"

Paige gave a dry laugh. "I'd have thought you'd have been thoroughly relieved," she said, but without rancor. "Now I've got a husband. It makes things . . . perfect." She glanced down at the diamond-studded wedding band Jesse had slipped onto her finger during the ceremony, and twisted it around.

"He has good taste," Laura remarked. "It's a beautiful ring."

"Umm. I think he's determined to let the world know that he's doing it right."

"Your father likes him."

"What's not to like? He's been the perfect gentleman." Indeed, he'd said and done all the right things. Of course, neither Laura nor Phillip had felt the formality of Jesse's hand when it curved around Paige's waist. Neither could they imagine how different his ceremonial kiss had been from the persuasive warmth of the kisses they'd shared at one time. "Do *you* like him, Mom?"

"Yes. Yes, I do. He's intelligent and well-spoken. You make a handsome couple. And, though you may object to my saying this, I think he's done the best thing. You're carrying his child and you have a right to his protection." She held up a hand as Paige opened her mouth. "I know. I know. You're perfectly capable of taking care of yourself. But, as a parent, I have to say I'm relieved that you won't have the pressure of shouldering it all on your own." Her gaze grew more worried. "I only wish you were happier about his return."

"I'm happy enough," Paige murmured, but her voice lacked conviction. She hadn't told her mother the details of her reunion with Jesse, had simply called to say they were getting married.

"Do you want to talk about it?" Laura asked softly.

"Talk about it?"

"Your concerns. Things aren't exactly hunky-dory, are they?"

Strangely, Paige did want to talk. She'd felt so bottled up since Jesse's brusque declaration of intent that she needed desperately to talk. More, she needed her mother's encouragement that she'd been right in agreeing to the marriage.

"No, I wouldn't say hunky-dory is quite the word," she said sadly. "Jesse was furious when he found out I was pregnant. The last thing I expected him to do was to propose marriage." *Demand* was more the case, but it was irrelevant at this point.

"He seems happy enough about the baby now."

"Oh, yes. Funny, he came around very quickly on that issue. He's determined to give the child everything he never had, and I'm sure he'll do it." She remembered the way his voice had grown soft when he'd spoken of those things he'd do with his child. "I do think he'll love our child."

"But?"

The eyes Paige raised to her mother held a world of regret. "Whether he'll ever love *me* is another matter."

"You don't think he does?"

"At one point I might have thought so. There were times when he was here last summer when I might have imagined him to be in love. Then again, when he first saw me the other day, he was as excited as I was. That was before he learned about the baby. I'm not sure he'll ever forgive me for that."

Laura's voice grew exquisitely gentle. "Love doesn't just go away, darling. Even if he's angry at you right now, if the seeds of his love are there and you nurture them properly, they'll blossom."

"That's a pretty image," Paige argued sadly, "but it might just be wishful thinking when it comes to Jesse Dallas. Don't forget, this is a man who's fed on anger for better than thirty-five years."

"But from what you say, his mother never made the slightest attempt to give. That's where things may be different now. It could be that he just needs coaxing. It could be that he wants very much to love you, but that he's fighting it. All you have to do is persevere. I know you. You succeed when you set your mind to things."

"I know. I'm just not sure it'll work this time." Eyes clouded with pain, she wrapped her arms around her middle. "Jesse is so . . . remote when he looks at me, when he touches me. I may have gained a loving father for my child, but a loving husband?"

Laura paused then, cautiously studying her daughter's face. "You could have said no, Paige. Why did you agree to the marriage?"

Paige sighed and seemed to sink into the chair in defeat. The look she gave Laura was rife with helplessness. "I love him, Mom. It's as simple as that."

"Then you'll make it work, darling. Just keep at it. You'll make it work!"

HER MOTHER'S WORDS, and the love Paige did in fact feel, kept her going for a while. Jesse sold his New York town house, furniture and all, and moved the rest of his belongings to Marblehead. He set up his Kem machine in one of the spare bedrooms, which he'd allocated as his workroom, and fit back into Paige's daily existence in much the way he'd done the summer before . . . with several notable exceptions. The warmth was gone. The gentle companionship seemed strained. And, though they shared the same bed, he didn't attempt to make love to her. Not once.

Paige might have blamed the latter on his awareness of her condition, but he'd been right there when her doctor had okayed lovemaking. Right up until the last month, or until she was too uncomfortable, the doctor had said. But Paige was only in her fifth month and not physically uncomfortable at all, and still Jesse avoided her. He was punishing her. She was sure of it. And she let him have his way. All she could do was show him in small and subtle ways—a smile here, a special meal there, acquiescence, understanding—that she loved him. Beyond that, it was up to him.

Christmas came a short three weeks after their marriage and, though Paige had agonized over making the suggestion, Jesse was surprisingly agreeable to spending the holidays in Westport. Sure, he'd like to meet her brothers and their families, and wasn't it good of them all to come in so soon after the September bash? Sure, he'd like to see her parents again. Maybe he'd even try his hand at golf with her father—but no, the course would be closed for the winter. And yes, it'd be nice to see the house where she'd grown up.

Paige dreaded it, again because of the pretense. To have to behave like a loving couple before these people who meant so much to her was going to be difficult. Oh, she was loving enough. But Jesse?

As it happened, her fears were unfounded. For one thing—and she should have anticipated it—there was so much pandemonium in a house filled with ten adults and five children that Paige and Jesse as a couple were hardly noticeable. The youngsters were so high on the Christmas spirit that their enthusiasm took precedence over most else. For another thing—and this Paige hadn't dared anticipate—Jesse quite easily donned the facade of the loving husband. He held her hand, put his arm around her shoulder, smiled and laughed with her in a way that seemed utterly natural.

He got along fine with her brothers, too, and seemed comfortable without being patronizing. Their wives took to him as well, responding quite helplessly to his subtle charm. The children were more shy at first, but after the first snowball fight in the yard the boys were won over. And Paige would never forget his conquest of Sami, Michael's seven-year-old daughter. On the first day she eyed him from a distance. On the second, she began to position herself by his side whenever possible. On the third, she approached the chair in which he was seated, stood staring at him for endless moments, then whispered, for only his ears and Paige's, who sat on the arm of his chair, "You've got pretty eyes." He'd broken into a smile then and had hoisted her onto his knee, which became her near-constant perch from then on.

Even in the privacy of Paige's bedroom, when she and Jesse were getting ready for bed at night or getting dressed in the morning, Jesse seemed less restrained.

"Uncle Jesse," he repeated, smiling. "I never imagined what I was getting when I married you."

"Are you sorry?" she asked, and was pleased when he confirmed her suspicion.

"Nah. It's fun. They're great kids. And I like their parents."

Still he made no attempt to make love to Paige, and while she sensed that her family had scored points, she felt that she'd scored few. The drive back to Marblehead was made largely in silence. By the time they were inside their oceanfront home once again, Jesse was as aloof as ever.

January came and Paige entered her sixth month of pregnancy. Her stomach was rounding nicely, and she'd gained some weight, though not as much as the doctor wished.

"You're eating properly, aren't you, good healthy things?" she asked at Paige's monthly appointment.

Jesse answered quickly. "She's got all those things on her plate, but she usually leaves half of what's there."

The doctor cast a glance Paige's way. "You shouldn't, you know. You're eating for two."

"I know," she said softly, intimidated with Jesse sitting so imperiously by her side. She wished he'd let her see the doctor alone, but when she suggested it he simply set his jaw and shook his head. He didn't trust her. That much was certain. "I'm just . . . not that hungry. And I feel worse if I stuff myself."

"By all means don't stuff yourself, but you should try to eat enough. Perhaps you ought to have four or five smaller meals a day."

Paige cringed then, and with good cause. From that time on, Jesse himself presented her with those four or five meals, then stood by while she struggled to swallow. She tried her best, both to eat and to indulge him his protectiveness, but, increasingly, his protectiveness stifled her, particularly as it lacked the warmth she craved.

In the end, when she simply couldn't stomach another bite, they'd argue.

"I can't, Jesse."

"It's for the child. The one you wanted so badly. If you starve it, it'll be no good to either one of us."

"Then *you* eat for it," she snapped, eyes flashing. It took a lot to get her goat, but days on end of Jesse's remoteness had begun to tie her in knots.

"My eating won't do it any good, or believe me I'd do it. As it is, I'm doing everything I can to make sure it's healthy, which is a hell of a lot more than you're doing. You won't nap during the day. You barely sleep at night."

"How would you know that? You sleep like a baby yourself!"

"I know. Believe me, I know. Your tossing and turning wakes me up and I can tell from your breathing that you're not asleep."

"If I'm bothering you," she goaded, "try another bedroom." She'd been pushing to rile him, but she didn't succeed. Jesse simply walked away from her. And he was back in his place in bed that night.

He was playing a game, she decided. It was part of her punishment. His concern for the well-being of the child she carried knew no bounds, but the very contrast between that and his concern for her own emotional well-being was dramatic. At times he'd walk through a room and barely glance at her. Conversation between them was sparse, making meals a horror for Paige even beyond the effort to eat. When he'd appear at nine o'clock and tell her to go to bed, she went, if only to escape the ever-present chasm that stretched between them.

As soon as he could after moving his things, Jesse took on an editing assignment and spent hours holed up with his machine, emerging only to see to those needs of hers that related to the child. Paige, on the other hand, did little sculpting, finding herself more often than not staring at a piece of stone without the slightest idea of what to carve or where to begin. If she'd hoped to find salvation in her work, it failed her, too. She could only pray that once the baby was born, inspiration would return.

During those evenings that they actually spent together in the living room, Jesse was preoccupied studying the baby books she'd bought or one of those he'd subsequently picked up himself. He appeared to be taking a disciplined approach to not only pregnancy and childbirth, but child rearing itself, wanting to know every fact, every possibility, every recommendation.

On occasion, she'd find his gaze wandering to her, his eyes settling on her stomach, or on her ankles, propped on the coffee table. At those times, she'd feel her heart lift in the hope that maybe he'd soften, but no sooner did he catch her hopeful eye than he looked away.

It was like that from time to time in bed, too. She'd awaken in the morning, groggy from a shallow and disturbed sleep, to find his arm around her waist, his hand on her stomach. The latter wasn't unusual; he'd taken his turn at feeling the movement of the baby, but his touch had never strayed to the sexual. These early-morning touches were different, as though it was her flesh he wanted. But she'd no sooner reach to cover his hand than he'd withdraw it. Once she even awoke to a more ardent caress; he was stroking her breasts while he buried his lips against her neck. This time she was careful, holding her breath, afraid to turn or respond lest she anger him. She needed him so badly; her pregnancy had done little to dull that urge. But it was to go unsated. His fingers wandered, grew bolder . . . then abruptly withdrew and he rolled to the far side of the bed. She was never to know if he'd reached for her in his sleep; if that had been the case, she might have had the hope that a subconscious part of him wanted her, needed her as much as she very consciously wanted and needed him. But his detachment the following morning thwarted her hopes.

He was taunting her, tormenting her. Aching, she'd grit her teeth and try to be grateful for his fleeting caresses, but it became apparent that regardless of what his body felt or did, his mind was set strongly against her. She began, in the long periods of idleness when her hands couldn't seem to find their way around a chisel or file, to imagine what the future would be like. It wasn't a pretty picture. She saw days stretching into weeks, months, then years during which she and Jesse would share a home and a child, go through the motions of marriage with none of the feeling. She wondered if he'd *ever* make love to her again, wondered if he'd seek out other women as he'd done when he'd gone back to New York. She didn't think she could bear that, and found herself agonizing over thoughts of an eventual divorce . . . but only until she reminded herself of his threat. Joint custody. Her child gone from her for fully half of the year. *That* would destroy her. It was bad enough that Jesse rejected the love she tried to give, but if he were to deny her the only other outlet she'd have, she thought she'd die.

By February, Paige was beginning to feel heavy. Her stomach seemed to stick straight out in front of her—a sure sign of a boy, was the consensus of her mother's bridge group. And there were times—the doctor said they were perfectly normal—when she experienced contractions and her stomach grew rock hard. She'd curve her hand under it for support then and continue with what she was doing. Inevitably, Jesse would be at her in a minute.

"Sit down, Paige. Give it a chance to pass."

"My making dinner won't hurt."

"You don't have to rough it. These aren't the Dark Ages when women worked in the fields, squatted to give birth, then stood right up and went back to work again."

If he'd spoken with concern, she might have listened. But his even tone told another story. In defiance, she'd continue what she was doing until the spasm passed, *then* she'd settle listlessly into a chair. Inevitably, too, he'd berate her for her lack of concern for the baby. One day, when he did, she lashed back with uncharacteristic curtness. Heartsick and exasperated, she felt she'd begun to teeter on the perilous tightrope she walked.

"Get off my case, Jesse. I'd do much better if you'd leave me alone."

"If I left you alone, God only knows what you'd do to my kid!"

"That's not fair. I was doing beautifully until you came along."

"That was before the baby started making demands. It's easy enough to do beautifully when there's nothing to do. Now, though, you've got to eat right and watch that you don't overdo things."

"*Overdo things?* You don't let me do *anything!*" She lowered her voice, feeling dangerously close to tears, and spoke as though to herself. "I think I'm going crazy. I feel cooped up and frustrated. It's been so cold that I can't go anywhere, and now I look forward to each doctor's appointment as if it's a party."

The doctor didn't feel quite that way when she saw Paige several weeks later. Concluding her examination, she remained by Paige's side to talk with her quietly while Jesse went out to the outer office.

"Is something bothering you, Paige?"

"Bothering me?"

"You're dragging. You look exhausted. Your blood pressure's up. And you're still not gaining the weight you should."

Paige's eyes widened in fear. "Is something wrong? With the baby?"

The doctor smiled kindly. "No, no. The baby sounds fine. Its heartbeat is good and strong. *It* seems to be growing well, but I think it's taking its weight pound for pound from you."

"That's all right. I can afford to be slimmer."

"No, you can't. My concern is for both baby and mother. And you don't seem happy. At least, not the way you were at the start of your pregnancy."

Paige wrinkled up her nose and tried to make light of the observations. "Oh, I'm sure it's just impatience. Nine months seems like such a long time sometimes."

"True. But . . . somehow I didn't think you'd be one to wither under the pressure."

"I'm not withering."

"That's what it looks like to me." She took a breath and spoke with supreme gentleness. "I may be overstepping my bounds here, Paige, but as I said, my concern is as much for you as for your baby. I'm not blind, or deaf. Speaking as one woman to another, I can see the tension between you and your husband. And I do know that the marriage didn't take place until well into the pregnancy. If you want to talk, and I think it might do you good, I'd be glad to lend an ear."

Paige looked away, then closed her eyes and sighed wearily. "I don't think it'll do any good. Jesse wants the baby. It's me he doesn't want."

"That's not what I see. I see a man who's genuinely concerned for you both. Oh, maybe he gets a little carried away, but I think his heart's in the right place."

"Could've fooled me."

"You're not looking as objectively as I am. You have to realize that a man is at his most helpless when his wife is pregnant." When Paige opened her mouth to disagree, the doctor went on quickly. "You're doing all the work. He feels left out. Some men have to compensate by trying their best to take control of the situation."

"He's succeeded."

"Obviously not, since your health leaves something to be desired. And if you don't do something to improve that, the baby may well be endangered at some point. You know, Paige, I'm great at giving advice like this, but I'm not a counselor. I do know of several good ones, if you'd be interested."

Oh, yes, she'd be interested. *Anything* to break though the barrier Jesse had created. But she doubted *he'd* go for that. He wasn't even willing to admit that a problem existed! From all outward signs, he seemed satisfied with the status quo.

"Uh . . . well, let me discuss it with Jesse," she murmured, doubting she would but needing to appease the doctor somehow. "If we decide to go ahead, I'll give you a call for the referral."

"Will you?"

Paige nodded. From the look in the doctor's eye, though, she knew she hadn't fooled her for a minute.

"And will you try to take better care of yourself? Eat well? Get lots of rest? Keep calm? You're going to have to work things out before that little one is born. It won't be any easier then."

"I know," Paige whispered, feeling more discouraged than ever.

After leaving the office, she thought long and hard about the doctor's suggestion that she and Jesse see a counselor. But she *knew* what was wrong; it was no mystery. Jesse had chosen to put a distance between them. He refused to share himself with her as he'd once done. He resented her. He was angry. That very anger would rule out the possibility of counseling. And the worst of it was that . . . she didn't even dare ask.

She wondered what had become of the self-confident woman she'd been several months before. For that matter, Paige hardly recognized herself. The zest she'd had for life was gone, as was the optimism, the determination. She'd tried to break through Jesse's shield during the first months of their marriage. She'd tried to be patient and understanding, to show the love she didn't dare express in words, knowing that he'd surely laugh in her face. Finally, she'd given up. She was just too tired, too heartsick to make the exertion.

It was a side of herself she'd never seen before. True, Jesse Dallas had chipped away her cool exterior to reveal the passionate woman beneath, but when he'd chipped further—as he'd been doing these past weeks— he'd hit flaws. One after the other. Weaknesses Paige hadn't known existed. And as disgusted as she was with herself, she didn't know where to turn. For her parents, the doctor, any friends who happened by, she managed to put on a passable facade. After all, she'd made her bed; now she had to sleep in it. But alone once more she was drained. Nothing seemed to matter…nothing except the baby. And though she did her best to eat and sleep well, it was never enough. It appeared that she was letting the baby down, too.

Jesse kept himself busy, finishing one job, starting another with the expressed intention of taking time off after the baby's birth. Paige should have been relieved by his noble stand, but she wasn't. For hours she'd sit alone with a book in her lap, feeling lonesome, wishing desperately for company. When she'd bound up in frustration and begin to pace the room, she'd be stopped either by a sharp pain in her hip—the baby was pressing on a nerve, the doctor said—or a wave of dizziness. This she didn't even *report* to the doctor. So she'd sit down again, limp and discouraged. When she finally heard Jesse emerge from his workroom, she'd begin to tremble not in pleasure but in apprehension.

One afternoon early in March she could take it no longer. Jesse had gone off to pick up groceries, insisting that she take a nap while he was gone. But she didn't want to nap, and she was sure that if she sat in the house alone for one minute longer she'd truly lose her mind.

Wearing a stylish wool jumper, boots, and her oversize winter coat, she headed for the garage. She couldn't remember the last time she'd driven her car. Jesse was adamant about taking her everywhere she wanted to go. But all along the doctor had told her she could drive, and she had every intention of doing so now.

Sliding behind the wheel became her first major obstacle. When last she'd been in the driver's seat, she'd been much slimmer. Grunting, she leaned forward, tugged at the lever and moved the seat back, then patted her stomach and sighed. She extended the seat belt, then let it slide back, fearing that it would do the baby more potential harm than good. Backing the car carefully from the garage and onto the road, she put it in gear. That was when she faced her second obstacle.

Where to go. If she went into Marblehead, chances were strong she might pass Jesse on the way. He'd try to make her go back, and she wouldn't! She just wouldn't! She needed these few minutes of freedom as badly as she'd ever needed anything. Taking her only other option, she headed away from Marblehead center and drove along the shore route.

After a while she began to feel warm in her coat, and she tried shrugging out of it. But her bulky clothing worked against her so she finally gave up and simply rolled down her window. The air retained its crispness but was milder than it had been in weeks. Her thoughts raced ahead toward the first of May, when her baby was due, and she imagined herself pushing a carriage, breathing in the warm ocean air once more, admiring nature's rebirth even as she displayed her own offspring proudly.

Before she knew it, she was on the road to Boston. Yes, she felt like going there. Perhaps she'd park and walk along Newbury Street, maybe even stroll through the stores examining the clothes she'd buy when she was her old svelte self once more. She'd be gone for several hours, maybe more, and if Jesse worried, so what! He deserved it, overbearing ape that he'd been! Let him stew, just as she'd been doing since the day he'd so rudely reappeared in her life.

Her third obstacle, though, was her own fatigue. She began to feel it on the outskirts of the city as the traffic picked up, and it grew steadily worse. Stopped at a traffic light, she managed at last to peel off her coat, but she felt little relief when it lay bunched on the seat beside her.

When had she grown so weak? Weren't pregnant women supposed to be endowed with some kind of divine strength? She broke out in a sweat, and when her limbs began to quiver, she thought back on what she'd eaten that day. Breakfast, a midmorning snack, lunch—each meal had been scanty, but she'd eaten no less than normal. That wasn't saying much; possibly it explained her shakiness.

Following the ramp over North Station onto Storrow Drive, she drove until she reached the Arlington Street exit, determined to park and visit the first coffee shop she found.

She never made it. Somewhere alongside the Public Garden, with her foot on the gas and her hands on the wheel, she passed out cold.

RETURNING TO THE HOUSE with several bags of groceries and a book for Paige, Jesse went directly to the kitchen to put the food away. He was grateful that she had taken his suggestion and was sleeping. Damn, but she'd been hard to handle lately. Quite a change from the self-possessed, easygoing woman he'd known the summer before, but then, she was pregnant and having quite a time of it. It was a damn good thing he'd come back when he had; no telling how she'd *ever* have managed on her own!

Storing a carton of milk on the refrigerator shelf, he ran his hand down its damp surface and, frowning, thought ahead to the future. He wondered what would happen when the baby was born, whether things would thaw between Paige and himself. True, they'd have the child as a diversion, but there still remained the matter of their own relationship.

He'd been hard on her. He knew that. So perhaps he was as much at fault as she. Yes, she'd deceived him by getting pregnant, but she hadn't asked that he marry her, or that he take care of her as he'd done these past months. He'd been angry. He still was. He felt manipulated into something he'd have sworn he hadn't wanted.

And yet . . . there were times when he imagined it might actually work. He'd seen her family, witnessed the warmth firsthand, and had dared to dream that one day he and Paige might have that, too. Oh, he wanted the baby. He'd never have believed how much. And, yes, he wanted Paige, too. But he wanted that other Paige, the one she'd been before—so independent that every show of affection on her part was a special gift.

She had been affectionate. He remembered each and every gesture. He could have sworn that she loved him...until lately. Lately she hadn't cared much about anything. Lately she'd been without self-assurance, without direction, losing interest even in sculpting. Lately she'd cringed every time he'd walked into the room. Had he done that to her? Had he pushed her too far?

She had no way of knowing that many of the hours in his workroom he spent thinking, wondering, worrying. She had no way of knowing that he felt guilty about things that he wished could be different, that the tension between them was taking a toll on him, too.

For indeed it was. He was confused. And frightened. Frightened to reach out for something that would mean the world to him, frightened of taking that risk and then somehow, sometime, losing. For years it had seemed better to go his own way.

The baby had changed all that. He was committed in one sense. No, he was committed in a far greater sense. Paige was his wife. They were legally married...at *his* insistence. Perhaps that was one of the things that made him uneasy. If she'd come to him of her own free will, perhaps he'd feel more confident where she was concerned.

There were nights when he'd yearned to reach out for her, nights when he had, then pulled back. He was a coward. So what in the hell was he going to do about it? God, he didn't know!

Wearily he stowed the rest of the groceries, folded the empty bags and stored them, then picked up the book and went to check on Paige. At the bedroom door he stopped. The bed was empty, as smooth and neatly made as it had been that morning.

"Paige?" Perhaps she was in the bathroom. He walked to its door. "Paige?" No Paige. Turning, he retraced his steps, calling her name at each door, hearing nothing in return. He searched each room in the wing, then stalked toward the other wing. "Paige! Where are you?"

Her studio was empty, as was his workroom and the guest bedroom. "Damn it, where are you?" he growled to himself as he ran back to the living room and looked out toward the deck. There was no sign of her anywhere. Angrily he slid open the glass door and stepped outside, then crossed the deck and trotted down toward the beach. The snow was gone, but it was cold. Ignoring the chill he felt, he looked first one way then the other, then took off across the sand.

"Paige! Paige!" His voice was caught and swallowed by a wind that seemed as angry as he. Grinding to a halt, he cupped his mouth and yelled, "Paiiiiige!" When no answer came, he ran until the rocks bid him stop, then turned and loped in the other direction. "Goddammit, Paige! Paiiiiige!"

Within minutes, he concluded that she wasn't on the beach. Bounding back up the steps and through the house, he stormed into the garage. *"Goddammit!"* She'd taken her car.

Returning to the kitchen for his keys and coat, he took his own car and headed for town. All the way he simmered. All the way he railed aloud as though Paige were sitting in the passenger's seat. "Of all the crazy stunts! Damn it, you could have told me you wanted to go out! I'd have taken you! So what if you don't get the rest you need! So what if you catch pneumonia! So what if you kill the baby! All right, be selfish if you want! But, God, don't walk out on me this way!"

For the next two hours, he scoured not only Marblehead but also Salem and Beverly, searching all her favorite shops, even those she'd visited less frequently. When the stores had pretty much closed for the day he headed home, keeping such a sharp eye out for her car that he nearly rear-ended one himself.

By the time he arrived back at the house, it was nearly six and dark. He ran from his car to check the garage, then swore vehemently when it was empty. But there was a touch of panic in his tone now, and he dashed into the house and headed for the phone.

By some miracle he managed to keep his voice calm as he called each of her friends in the area. Paige had gone out for a drive and had she, by chance, stopped there? He asked over and over again. But to no avail. No one had seen her. No one had heard from her. For the first time he realized just how much of a recluse she'd become in the past weeks, and he wondered whether to blame it on her condition or on *him*. He hadn't encouraged her to see her friends. What had he said when she'd seemed restless? *Take a nap. It'll do you good.*

It was his fault, damn it! His fault!

But self-reproach would have to wait. Frantic now, he tried to think of where she might have gone. Had she been depressed enough to run home to her parents? A quick forage through her dresser told him that she hadn't packed for an overnight stay, and her suitcase was in the storage closet.

As the minutes crept by, he cursed his helplessness. Fleeting images began to haunt him—images of her having just picked up and taken off with no other goal in mind than escape. He didn't blame her. Damn his stubbornness! If she'd been frozen out, he'd done it single-handedly. She had every right to hate him for the way he'd behaved! He could have showed a little compassion for what she felt. He could have tried to talk with her, to express his feelings, to air his frustration and anger and fear.

Frustration and anger were forgotten now. Only fear remained, and it grew and grew as he struggled to decide what to do. He didn't realize he was sweating until he raked his hand through his hair and found it damp. He tried to think clearly, to keep calm, but it grew harder as the clock ticked on. She'd taken the car, so he couldn't suspect foul play. But what if she'd had a flat, or run out of gas, or . . . or . . .

Doing the only thing left to be done, he picked up the phone to call the police. He'd barely punched out the exchange, though, when the doorbell rang. Slamming the phone back down, he raced for the door. Maybe she'd forgotten her key. Maybe she was just too tired to put it in the lock.

But it wasn't Paige whose finger was about to press the bell a second time. It was one of the very same men he'd been about to call.

"Mr. Dallas?"

His heart seemed to stop, his life suspended. "Yes?" he asked in a fleeting breath.

"We've been trying to reach you. First there was no answer. Then the line was busy. So I thought I'd—"

"What is it, man?"

"Your wife. I'm afraid there's been an accident. . . ."

10

Never in his life had Jesse been so terrified. He felt as though his world were about to shatter, as though if he could only put his arms around it, he might hold it together. But his arms were useless; there was nothing to grasp. He had to reach for that world, had to reach for it. . . .

Refusing the policeman's offer of a ride into Boston, he drove his own car at a breakneck pace, running red lights whenever possible in his haste to reach Paige.

The policeman had said she was all right, but what did *he* know? She'd fainted at the wheel and had banged her head when the car had gone into a streetlight. Concussion? Skull fracture? Blood clot in the brain?

Jesse was shaking all over by the time he made it to the emergency room. But Paige had already been admitted, so he had to suffer the wait for an elevator, then the ride to the sixth floor before finally bolting out toward the desk.

The nurse on duty was on the phone, but Jesse was too panicked to wait politely. "Excuse me, but my wife's just been admitted." The nurse continued her conversation, though she did eye him. "Dallas. Paige Dallas. Could you tell me where she is? I've just found out about her accident. I've got to see her."

"Mr. Dallas?"

Jesse's head shot up as a resident approached from behind the desk and extended a hand. "I'm Dr. Brassle. I'll be keeping an eye on your wife."

The hand Jesse placed in the doctor's was boneless and cold, his voice little more than a fearful gasp. "How is she?"

The doctor smiled. "She'll be fine. Just a mild concussion. But she's very weak. I assume this pregnancy's been hard on her."

"Pregnancy..." Jesse murmured. In his panic about Paige, he hadn't even thought about the baby. When he raised stricken eyes, the doctor was still smiling.

"The baby's fine. Evidently has no intention of making an early appearance. I'd like to keep your wife here for a few days' rest and observation, though."

"A mild concussion?"

"That's all. We took a few stitches, and she's apt to have a good headache for a while, but there's no sign of any deeper problem."

Jesse sagged in relief. "Thank God," he whispered. "Can I see her now?"

"Sure. Room 604. She was very shaky, so we gave her a mild sedative—for the baby's sake more than anything—but we don't want her to sleep long. The nurse will be around every few minutes to make sure she's all right."

"Thank you." Jesse was already starting off. "Room 604?"

The doctor nodded, gesturing broadly down the hall.

It took Jesse a minute to find it, then he stopped to catch his breath and still his hammering pulse before going in.

Her eyes were closed, her face frighteningly pale. A small piece of gauze was taped high on her brow. He approached quietly, flexing his fingers by his sides. He wanted to touch her. God, he *had* to touch her. He had to know that she was all right. He had to tell her he was sorry. He had to tell her that he . . . that he . . .

Raising a hand to her cheek, he brushed it lightly. It was cool, so cool. Should it be that cool? He wanted to race out to ask the doctor, but couldn't bear the thought of leaving her side.

Pulling a chair close to the bed, he sat down, took her hand in both of his and raised it to his lips. He'd will her to be all right. He'd will her back into the woman who'd taken his heart. Damn it, she didn't have a right to do this to him! She didn't have a right to tear down every defense he'd built and then just . . . just take off!

When she took a deep breath, he froze. Slowly she turned her head, even more slowly opened her eyes. It seemed to take her a minute to focus, then her eyes widened. "Jesse?" She barely mouthed the words.

"It's all right, love. I'm here."

She swallowed hard, and her momentary calm seemed to crumble. Her whisper was tremulous. "I'm...I'm sorry, Jesse...oh, God, I didn't mean to do that . . ."

"Shhhhhhhh." He breathed against her fingers, which clutched his with surprising strength.

"I didn't mean..." Her eyes filled with tears. "I didn't...I'm so sorry..."

The tears were streaming down her cheeks then, and Jesse's insides turned. He'd never seen her cry. Not once through what had to have been a months-long ordeal for her had she cried. But she did now, and he realized the full extent of what he'd done.

Shifting to sit on the bed, he gathered her very gently in his arms. "Shhhh. Don't cry, love. God, don't cry." He tried to be tender holding her, but his arms tightened in need. He buried his face in her hair, aware that his own breath was coming in ragged gasps. "I can't bear to see you cry, Paige. I need your strength. Without it I'm nothing."

Through her sobs she barely heard what he was saying. "Ohhh...Jesse...I should have listened...I'm sorry...I'm sorry..."

"Please, baby, don't cry. Don't cry." He rubbed her back, frightened by the slenderness that contrasted so much with her fullness in front. "I'm the one who's sorry. I drove you out. It's my fault. All my fault."

He continued to caress her, to breathe in the sweet smell of her hair, to feel her warm and pliant in his arms as he thought she might never be again. Paige tried to control her tears, but they flowed on as though from a dam that had burst. Jesse's nearness, his touch, so wonderfully sweet, only added to the flow.

"Shhhhh. It's all right. Shhhhh." Closing his eyes, Jesse knew he'd been given a gift. Paige was all right. She was here. She was holding him. Burrowing his face more deeply against her neck, he moaned, "God, I . . . love you . . ."

Paige caught her breath on a sob, unsure if she'd only imagined his hoarse whisper because she'd wanted so badly to hear those words. Blotting her eyes against his shoulder, she gripped his arms and pulled back. Her eyes held uncertainty, disbelief, hope. "Wh-what did you say?" she breathed unsteadily, then reached up in awe to touch the damp rivulets on his cheeks.

"I've made a mess of this whole thing, Paige," he managed. His gaze was blurred and he wanted nothing more than to bury his face against her until he'd composed himself. But there was much to be said, and since she'd already seen his tears . . . "I know I've put you through hell these months, but I've been there and back myself today." He took a shaky breath. "It's been hard for me . . . accepting all this because . . . it's contrary to everything I thought I wanted in life. But when I was racing around in a panic, not knowing where you were or whether you were hurt or even alive, I realized that what I thought I wanted just won't work anymore. I used to think that the real hell in life would be loving and losing, so I refused to be vulnerable. With you, I couldn't help it. I ran off last summer because I was scared, but I couldn't stay away. I guess I compensated by denying what I felt, by striking back, by trying my best to kill what I thought might hurt me. But the real hell of it is that I hurt anyway. The thought that I'd lost you today even before I'd given that love a chance nearly killed me."

He paused to brush the tears from her cheek, aware of the astonishment on her face. "I know I haven't got a right to ask this of you. You must hate me for everything I've done. But . . ." His voice softened, trembling still. "But I'd like another chance, Paige. I'd like another chance to show how much I. . .I love you. Maybe in time you could. . .could love me again?"

"I do."

Jesse's heart flipped. It wasn't so much the two small words as the way she'd spoken them that sent him soaring. They were said calmly, factually, with the very same self-confidence that had captivated him from the start.

"You do?"

She nodded, suddenly imbued with a strength that overrode any effects of the sedative. "Love isn't something that starts and stops, Jesse. It's there. It doesn't go away. Even if you'd never come back after leaving in August, I'd have always loved you." Her eyes grew moist again. "For me the hell was in loving you and, day after day, having to face your disdain. I'm sorry I didn't tell you I wanted a baby—"

He stopped her words with one long finger. "Shhhh. Maybe you were right about that. I'd never have consented at the time. But it certainly forced the issue, and I do want that baby so badly."

"What about when it fusses and cries and disturbs your work? What about when we've got plans to go out and the baby-sitter cancels at the last minute? What about when we want to get away for a few days?"

"When it fusses, I'll rock it to sleep. When the sitter cancels, we'll call another. When we want to get away, we'll run it down to Westport. You've had the answers all along. I'm the one who always sees the dark side. And I'm not saying that I can change overnight. The fears of a lifetime aren't easy to erase. But I'll try. Damn it, Paige, I'll try. And if you'd be willing to help . . ."

The look of joy on her face took willingness one step further. Wrapping her arms around him, she pressed her newly glowing cheek to his chest as his arms made the circle complete.

That was how the nurse found them when she poked her head in a few minutes later. Smiling in satisfaction that her patient was on the mend, she quietly left.

EIGHT WEEKS LATER Paige and Jesse were in much the same position. It was a different bed, a different hospital, a different occasion, but their embrace was no less firm, their hearts no less filled with joy.

"She's beautiful, Paige. Just like you."

"Kinda red and wrinkled, don't you think?"

"Nah. Did you see those tiny fingers?"

"Uh-huh. All ten."

"God, they're cute. I think she's ticklish. When I touch the bottom of her feet, her toes curl."

"That's instinct."

"And her mouth . . . have you ever seen anything so sweet? All pink and puckering . . ."

"It is sweet, isn't it?"

"She's a winner, that's for sure. I called your parents. They're out of their minds with excitement!"

"Ahh, I knew they would be."

"They couldn't wait to call your brothers. I also called Sandy and Frank and Tom and Margie and Ben, who, by the way, said he can't win where I'm concerned. He bet on a boy."

"Poor Ben. Did you tell him how hard you worked?"

"You bet. If it hadn't been for me, you'd never have known when to stop breathing deeply and start panting."

"Mmm. Women are pretty helpless in situations like these."

"Okay, okay. So you could've managed. But it was me who would have felt helpless if I'd been stuck outside pacing the floors. I still can't believe it. When the top of her head appeared . . ."

"I think you saw more than I did. You'll have to tell me about it sometime."

Staring into Paige's adoring eyes, Jesse shook his head in wonder. "Our baby's got so much going for her. She's a lucky little girl."

"*We're* lucky. Does it scare you?"

"A little. I never dreamed I could be so happy. Thank you, Paige."

"Thank *you*, Jesse."

Just then the crib in which their daughter lay was wheeled in by a beaming nurse. The baby was making herself and her needs well-known. Jesse and Paige both looked her way, then looked back at each other and laughed in delight. Popping a warm kiss on Paige's brow, Jesse stood to rescue his daughter and deliver her to her mother.

SLOW BURN
Heather Graham Pozzessere

Faced with the brutal murder of her
husband, Spencer Huntington demands
answers from the one man who should have
them—David Delgado—ex-cop, her
husband's former partner and best
friend…and her former lover.

Bound by a reluctant partnership, Spencer
and David find their loyalties tested by
desires they can't deny. Their search for the
truth takes them from the glittering world of
Miami high society to the dark and
dangerous underbelly of the city—while
around them swirl the tortured secrets and
desperate schemes of a killer driven to
commit his final act of violence.

"Suspenseful…Sensual…Captivating…"
Romantic Times (USA)

MIRA

TEARS OF THE RENEGADE
Linda Howard

The world stopped for Susan Blackstone when she saw the stranger—and her heart stopped when she learned his name. He was Cord Blackstone, the black sheep of the family, and her own cousin by marriage.

Cord had come back for just one reason: revenge. But he hadn't counted on Susan any more than she had counted on him. Searing passion became the wild card in the battle for control of the family business— and it was too soon to know who had been dealt the winning card.

"You can't just read one Linda Howard!"

Catherine Coulter

MIRA

LOVE CHILD
Patricia Coughlin

It was no more than a stone's throw from
the million-dollar mansions of Newport's
privileged few to their servants' weathered
frame houses, but they were worlds apart.
And yet, the cold and elegant facade of
Newport society concealed a bitter secret
that linked two proud, troubled families
from those different worlds—and two
lovers too young to understand their shared
destiny. Their love was a decades-long
drama of desire and betrayal, played out
against the glittering backdrop of America's
most exclusive—and most heartless—
playground.

*"A talent of surpassing excellence,
Ms Coughlin is one of the truly unique
voices in the romance genre today."*

Romantic Times (USA)

MIRA

TEST OF TIME
Jayne Ann Krentz

HE MARRIED FOR THE BEST
REASON…
They had a lot in common and would be
great together in business—and in bed.
Marriage to Katy Randall would also help
make people forget just how rough Garrett
Coltrane's past had been.

SHE MARRIED FOR THE ONLY
REASON…
Love. But the growing fear that shook her
during the ceremony exploded into
heartbreak when she discovered that love
was the only thing Garrett didn't want.

DID THEY STAND A CHANCE AT
MAKING THE ONLY REASON THE
REAL REASON TO SHARE A
LIFETIME?

*"A master of the genre…nobody does it
better!"*

Romantic Times (USA)

MIRA

FIRE AND ICE
Diana Palmer

Like the heroine of one of her novels, bestselling author Margie Silver was willing to rise to Cal Van Dyne's challenge. The arrogant tycoon vowed that Margie's sister would never marry his brother; Margie was just as determined that the wedding would take place. Margie expected the worst from Cal—but not the cynical game of love he played with her on his lavish Florida estate. Suddenly Margie was gambling with her sister's future—and her own—with a dangerous adversary who made his own rules…until he met his match.

With over ten million copies of her books in print, Diana Palmer's readers treasure her emotional style. A gift for telling the most sensuous tales with charm and humour is Ms Palmer's trademark.

MIRA

CRUEL LEGACY
Penny Jordan

One man's untimely death deprives a wife of her husband, robs a man of his job and offers someone else the chance of a lifetime...

PHILIPPA RYECART—when her comfortable, sheltered world collapsed around her, she was not prepared to play the grieving widow.

JOEL BRUTON—with his job on the line, he hungered for emotional—and physical—comfort. He was to find consolation in an unexpected alliance.

SALLY BRUTON—with the role of family breadwinner forced upon her, she was tragically unaware of her husband's need for her, although she *was* susceptible to another man's flattering attention.

DEBORAH FRANKLIN—young and impetuous, she was ready to move up the career ladder. But was there any truth in her lover's accusations that her promotion was based less on merit than on the fact that her womanising boss desired her?

One death touches all these lives. How well will each of them survive such a *Cruel Legacy*...?

MIRA